Favorite Stories from
from
Cowgirl Kate
and Cocoa

Favorite Stories from Cowgirl Kate and Cocoa

Written By **Erica Silverman**

Painted By **Betsy Lewin**

sandpiper

Green Light Readers

Houghton Mifflin Harcourt

Boston   New York

First Green Light Readers edition, 2013

All rights reserved. Published in the United States by Sandpiper,
an imprint of Houghton Mifflin Harcourt Publishing Company.
Originally published as selections in *Cowgirl Kate and Cocoa* by Harcourt Children's Books,
an imprint of Houghton Mifflin Harcourt Publishing Company, 2005.

SANDPIPER and the SANDPIPER logo are trademarks of
Houghton Mifflin Harcourt Publishing Company.

Green Light Readers and its logo are trademarks of
Houghton Mifflin Harcourt Publishing Company,
registered in the United States of America and/or its jurisdictions.

For information about permission to reproduce selections from this book,
write to Permissions, Houghton Mifflin Harcourt Publishing Company,
215 Park Avenue South, New York, New York 10003.

www.hmhbooks.com

The display type was hand lettered by Georgia Deaver.
The text type was set in Filosofia Regular.
The illustrations in this book were done in watercolors
on Strathmore one-ply Bristol paper.

The Library of Congress has cataloged *Cowgirl Kate and Cocoa* as follows:
Silverman, Erica.
Cowgirl Kate and Cocoa/Erica Silverman, illustrated by Betsy Lewin.
p. cm.
ISBN: 978-0-15-202124-5 hardcover
ISBN: 978-0-15-205660-5 paperback
Summary: Cowgirl Kate and her cowhorse, Cocoa, who is always hungry,
count cows, share a story, and help each other fall asleep.
[1. Cowgirls—Fiction. 2. Horses—Fiction.]
I. Lewin, Betsy. Ill. II. Title.
Pz7.S58625Co 2005
[E]—dc22 2004005739

ISBN: 978-0-544-02268-3 paper over board
ISBN: 978-0-544-02267-6 paperback

Manufactured in China
SCP 10 9 8 7 6 5 4 3 2 1

4500400037

To Julio, the newest Torn —E.S.

To horses everywhere —B.L.

The Surprise

One morning
Cowgirl Kate brought a box
to the barn.

"What is in that box?" Cocoa asked.

"A surprise," said Cowgirl Kate.

"Sugar cookies?" he asked.

"A surprise," she said.

"Apple pie?" he asked.

"A surprise," she said.

"Give me my surprise!" he said.

"First eat your oats," she said.

Cocoa glared at the bucket.

He kicked it over.

Cowgirl Kate frowned.

"That was your breakfast," she said.

Cocoa snorted.

"I am done with my breakfast," he said.

"I want my surprise."

"First I must groom you,"
said Cowgirl Kate.
She curried him.

She brushed him.

Then she cleaned his hooves.

Cocoa stomped.
"I want my surprise now!"
He pushed open the box.
He took a big bite
of the surprise.
He chewed.
He swallowed.
"Yuck!" he said.
"This does not taste
good at all!"

"Of course not," said Kate.
"It is a hat."
   She put the hat on Cocoa's head
   and held up a mirror.
"Do you like it?" she asked.

Cocoa frowned.

"I have only two ears," he said.

"But this hat has three holes!"

Cowgirl Kate laughed.

"Next time," she said,

"eat your breakfast

and not your surprise."

Bedtime in the Barn

One night Cowgirl Kate slept in the barn.
"Good night, Cocoa," she said.
She crawled into her sleeping bag
and closed her eyes.

"Will you please fluff my straw?" Cocoa asked.

Cowgirl Kate sighed.

"I am very tired," she said.

But she climbed out of her sleeping bag
and fluffed his straw.
Then she crawled back into her sleeping bag.

"I am hungry," said Cocoa.

Cowgirl Kate sighed.

"You are always hungry," she said.

But she climbed out of her sleeping bag
and gave him three carrots.
Then she crawled back into her sleeping bag.

"Uh-oh! My water bin is low," said Cocoa.

Cowgirl Kate groaned.

"Why didn't you tell me that before?"

"I didn't think of it before," said Cocoa.

"First I was thinking about straw.

Then I was thinking about food.

Now I am thinking about water."

"You are doing too much thinking,"
said Cowgirl Kate.

But she climbed out of her sleeping bag
and filled up his water bin.

"Is there anything else?" she asked.

"No," said Cocoa.

"Good," she said.

"Now think about sleep!"

"Good night, Katie," said Cocoa.
"Good night, Cocoa," said Cowgirl Kate.

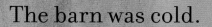

The barn was cold.
Cowgirl Kate pulled the sleeping bag
up to her chin.
The moon was bright.
She pulled the sleeping bag
over her eyes.

An owl hooted outside.

Whoooooo. Whoooooo.

Cowgirl Kate shivered.

"Cocoa! I cannot sleep," she said.

"Then I will sing you a lullaby," said Cocoa.

"Rock-a-bye, cowgirl,
on your cowhorse.
Though the wind blows,
you'll never be tossed.
When the dawn breaks,
your cowhorse will say,
'My hat's on. I'm ready
to herd cows all day.'"

And Cowgirl Kate smiled,
snuggled close . . .
and fell asleep.

Erica Silverman is the author of a series of books about Cowgirl Kate and Cocoa, the original of which received a Theodor Seuss Geisel Honor. She has also written numerous picture books, including the Halloween favorite *Big Pumpkin*, *Don't Fidget a Feather!*, *On the Morn of Mayfest*, and *Liberty's Voice.* Her new easy reader series, Lana's World, will be available from Green Light Readers soon. She lives in Los Angeles, California.

Betsy Lewin is the well-known illustrator of Doreen Cronin's *Duck for President; Giggle, Giggle, Quack;* and *Click, Clack, Moo: Cows That Type,* for which she received a Caldecott Honor. She lives in Brooklyn, New York.

QUICK REFERENCE

GUIDE TO

MICROSOFT®
WORD

FOR THE APPLE®MACINTOSH®

LISA ANN JACOBS

PUBLISHED BY
Microsoft Press
A Division of Microsoft Corporation
16011 NE 36th Way, Box 97017, Redmond, Washington 98073-9717

Library of Congress Cataloging in Publication Data

Jacobs, Lisa Ann.

Quick reference guide to Microsoft Word for the Apple Macintosh /
Lisa Ann Jacobs.

1. Microsoft Word (Computer program)   2. Macintosh (Computer)—
Programming.   3. Word processing.   I. Title.
Z52.5.M52J33   1989   89-3198
652'.5--dc19   CIP
ISBN 1-55615-209-4

Printed and bound in the United States of America.

1 2 3 4 5 6 7 8 9 WAKWAK 3 2 1 0 9

Distributed to the book trade in the United States by Harper & Row.

Distributed to the book trade in Canada by General Publishing
Company, Ltd.

Distributed to the book trade outside the United States and Canada
by Penguin Books Ltd.

Penguin Books Ltd., Harmondsworth, Middlesex, England
Penguin Books Australia Ltd., Ringwood, Victoria, Australia
Penguin Books N.Z. Ltd., 182-190 Wairau Road, Auckland 10,
New Zealand

British Cataloging in Publication Data available

Apple® and Macintosh® are registered trademarks of Apple Computer,
Inc. Microsoft® is a registered trademark of Microsoft Corporation.
PageMaker® is a registered trademark of Aldus Corporation.

Project Editor: Erin O'Connor
Technical Editor: Mary Ottaway

Introduction

You just purchased Microsoft Word 4 for the Apple Macintosh. It's a big, powerful program, but you don't have to thumb through hundreds of pages of manuals to produce your first professional-looking document.

With the help of this alphabetic, action-oriented reference guide, you can quickly produce the documents you need. You don't have to know the Word commands or options to find the information you need. You simply look up common terms like "Centering," "Graphics," or "Page numbers" as you would in a dictionary. The procedures you need are right there, or we tell you to *See:* another topic just a few pages away.

Each entry gives you all the information you need to complete a task, but only as much as you need. *See also:* notes refer you to related topics. By looking up the entry to read about only the topic you need, you save time and learn the Word features that are most important for completing your project.

After you've finished that crucial research paper or proposal, spend some time reading the entries you skipped and enhance your next project with other powerful Microsoft Word features.

If you're an old hand at Word and you already know the command name you need, turn to the Alphabetic Index to Commands at the back of the book to find the name of the entry that addresses the command. The Index to Menu Commands lists the menus alphabetically, shows you the commands on each menu, and directs you to the quick reference heading for each command. If you like using the keyboard instead of the mouse, refer to the appendix for keyboard equivalents.

If you are new to Microsoft Word, read these topics first: Starting Word, Opening a document, Typing text, Inserting text, Editing, Galley View, Page View, Print Preview, Formatting, Printing a document, and Saving a document.

Adding numbers

See: Math

Address labels

See: Mailing labels

Aligning paragraphs

To align paragraphs between left and right indents, select the paragraphs you want to align, choose the [Format] Show Ruler command to display the ruler, and click the appropriate alignment icon on the ruler. The alignment icons represent four types of alignment. From left to right, the alignment icons are for flush left, centered, flush right, and justified text.

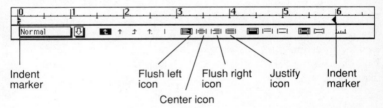

Indent marker · Flush left icon · Center icon · Flush right icon · Justify icon · Indent marker

Choosing the flush left icon aligns lines flush with the left indent but ragged at the right indent. Choosing the icon for centering centers lines between the left and right indents. Choosing the flush right icon aligns lines flush with the right indent but ragged at the left indent. Choosing the justify icon expands the spaces between words to align lines flush with both the left and the right indents.

Word aligns each paragraph between its left and right indents. To set indents for a paragraph, drag the indent markers to the desired positions on the ruler.

See also: Formatting paragraphs, Ruler

Alphabetizing

See: Sorting

Applying a style   *Shift-Command-S*

A style is a group of character, paragraph, section, and document formats to which you assign a name. After defining a style, you can apply it before typing a paragraph, or you can apply it to an existing
paragraph.

With keys

To apply a style before typing, position the insertion point at the beginning of the new paragraph and press Shift-Command-S. Type the
name of the style (the name appears in the lower-left corner of the
document window) and press the Return (or the Enter) key. Then type
the text for the paragraph.

To return to Normal style, press Shift-Command-S. Type *Normal* and
press the Return (or the Enter) key.

To apply a style to an existing paragraph, select the paragraph or posi-
tion the insertion point anywhere in the paragraph. Then press Shift-
Command-S, type the name of the style, and press the Return (or the
Enter) key.

With the ruler

To apply a style before typing, position the insertion point at the beginning of a new paragraph and choose the [Format] Show Ruler command. Choose the style name from the style box (shown below) and
then type the text for the paragraph.

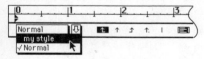

To apply a style to an existing paragraph, select the paragraph or position the insertion point anywhere in the paragraph. Then choose the
[Format] Show Ruler command and choose the style name from the
style box.

With the Styles command

If you aren't sure which style you want to apply, choose the [Format] Styles command to see a list of styles and their format definitions. Then select a style name from the list box and click the Apply button if you want to try out the style. Click OK to apply the style and close the dialog box.

Comments

After you apply a style to a paragraph, pressing the Return (or the Enter) key gives the next paragraph the same style. You can change the style of the next paragraph by specifying a style in the Next Style box of the [Format] Define Styles dialog box.

See also: Automatic styles, Defining a style, Next style, Selecting, Styles, Style sheets

Arithmetic

See: Math

ASCII files

See: Saving a document

Automatic styles

Automatic styles are styles predefined by Word. When you create a typical document element such as a header, footer, or page number, Word assigns an automatic style to it. For example, when you choose the [Document] Open Footer command to add a footer to a document, Word assigns the style *footer*, which consists of the *Normal* style with a 3-inch centered tab and a 6-inch flush right tab. In the [Format] Define Styles and Styles dialog boxes, automatic styles appear with bullets to their left.

To see all 33 automatic styles, hold down the Shift key and choose the [Format] All Styles or Define All Styles command.

Automatic styles *heading 1* through *heading 9* are directly tied to Outline View. For example, if you apply the *heading 1*, *heading 2*, and *heading 3* styles to titles in your document in Galley View, when you switch to Outline View with the [Document] Outlining command, each title will be indented according to its place in the outline's hierarchy. Any reorganizing you do affects both views.

To redefine an automatic style, choose the [Format] Define Styles command and select the automatic style you want to change from the list box. Choose new formats from the Format and Font menus or choose new settings from the ruler. Click the Define button to change the style for this document only, or click the Set Default button to use the redefined style as the default for all documents. Style definitions for automatic styles are stored in the Word Settings (4) file.

To return to Word's original automatic style definitions, delete the Word Settings (4) file from the Word Program disk or System folder and restart Word. When you restart, Word creates a new Word Settings (4) file with the file's original automatic style definitions. Note that deleting the Word Settings (4) file also deletes any other default settings you might have changed, such as options in the Preferences, Document, or Section dialog boxes.

Comments

All automatic styles are based on the *Normal* style, so if you change the definition of *Normal*, all automatic styles change accordingly.

See also: Applying a style, Outlining, Redefining a style, Styles, Style sheets, Word Settings (4) file

Basing one style on another

See: Style sheets

Boilerplate text

See: Glossary

Bold

See: Formatting characters

Borders

You can add borders to paragraphs and to tables or one or more cells of a table.

Paragraphs

To add a border to one or more paragraphs, first select the paragraph(s) and then choose the [Format] Paragraph command. Click the Borders button to open the Borders dialog box, select one of the five line styles (single, thick, double, dotted, or hairline), and select the Plain Box, Shadow Box, Outside Bar, or Custom option. Type a measurement in the Spacing: box if you want more than 2 points between the paragraph and the border. Click OK to close the Borders dialog box, and click OK to close the Paragraph dialog box.

Plain Box Draws a border around the outside of the selected paragraph(s).

Shadow Box Draws a border around the outside of the selected paragraph(s) and adds a shadow to the right and bottom edges.

Outside Bar Draws a border on the left edge of the selected paragraph(s).

Custom Draws a custom border when you click between the border
guides in the Borders dialog box to designate where you want each
edge to be drawn. To vary the line styles for individual edges, select
a different line style before clicking to add each edge.

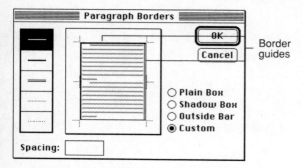

Spacing: Adds space between a paragraph and its border when you
type a measurement. The default spacing is 2 points.

To delete a border from one or more paragraphs, select the para-
graph(s) surrounded by the border and choose the [Format] Paragraph
command. Click the Borders button, choose the type of line that has
been used for the border, and click between the border guides to remove all the lines. With the exception of the Custom option, selecting
the option with which a border was created will also delete the border.
Click OK to close the Borders dialog box, and click OK to close the
Paragraph dialog box.

Tables and cells

To add a border around a table or to one or more cells, first select the
table (press the Option key and double-click) or the individual cells
that you want to border. Then choose the [Format] Cells command.
Click the Borders button to open the Borders dialog box and choose to
apply the border to the selected cells either as one block (a full border
will surround only the outside boundaries of the selection) or to every
cell in the selection (a full border will surround each cell in the selection). Click to select one of the five line styles (single, thick, double,
dotted, or hairline) and click between the border guides in the Borders
dialog box to add the border edges. Click OK to close the Borders dialog box, and click OK to close the Cells dialog box.

To delete borders from cells in a table, select the cells that have the
borders you want to delete and choose the [Format] Cells command.

Click the Borders button, choose the type of line that has been used for the border, and click between the border guides to remove all the lines. Click OK to close the Borders box, and click OK to close the Cells dialog box.

Comments
The hairline border style is always displayed on the screen as a single line and can be printed as a hairline only on a PostScript printer. On other printers, a hairline border prints as a single line. To display the current line style of a border, select the bordered paragraph or cells and choose the [Format] Paragraph or Cells command. Click the Borders button and hold down the Option key while you click between the border guides in the Borders dialog box. Word will select the current line style in the line-style selection box.

Canceling   *Command-period (.)*

You can cancel most operations in Word by clicking the Cancel button in the command's dialog box or by pressing the Escape key. If you've already clicked the OK button in a dialog box and want to stop a command in progress, press Command-period (.).

See also: Undoing

Cell formatting

See: Tables

Cells

See: Tables

Centering

See: Aligning paragraphs

Centimeters

See: Measurements

Changing a style

See: Redefining a style

Character formatting

See: Formatting characters

Chooser

Chooser is a Macintosh desk accessory (on the Apple menu). Use Chooser to indicate which printer you are using and the port it is connected to, or to connect to a printer on an AppleTalk network. You have to use Chooser to identify your printer only the first time you use Word or when you change printers. When changing printers, be sure you use Chooser to identify the new printer before paginating or laying out pages—page breaks and line breaks can vary from printer to printer.

The icons displayed in the Chooser window show the resources you have installed on the current System disk. To add or remove resources such as printer drivers, file servers, or other network devices, use Apple's utility program, Installer.

See also: Printing a document

Clearing

See: Deleting documents, Deleting tables and cells, Deleting text

Clipboard

The Clipboard is temporary storage for the text or graphics you last cut or copied with the [Edit] Cut or Copy command. To display the Clipboard's contents, choose the [Window] Show Clipboard command. You can move and size the Clipboard window the way you would any other window.

When you choose the [Edit] Paste command, Word inserts the Clipboard's contents at the insertion point. The contents stay on the Clipboard until you choose the [Edit] Cut or Copy command again, so you can paste the same text or graphics in more than one location.

When you quit Word, the Clipboard's contents are saved, so you can paste text or graphics into a document in another application. When the Clipboard is large, Word asks if you want to save the contents. Word saves the Clipboard's contents in a file called Clipboard File, usually in the System folder. When transferring data between applications, you might have to move the Clipboard File to the disk that holds the other application.

To cut and paste more than one item at a time, use the Scrapbook.

See also: Copying formats, Copying text, Moving text, Scrapbook

Closing a document   *Command-W*

To close a document, click the close box in the upper-left corner of the window or choose the [File] Close command. If you close a document with unsaved changes, Word asks if you want to save changes before closing. Click Yes to save changes and close the document, click No to discard changes and close the document, or click Cancel to return to editing the document.

See also: Deleting documents, Quitting Word, Saving a document

Color

See: Formatting characters

Columns

You can create two types of columns with Word: snaking columns or side-by-side columns.

Snaking columns

Snaking columns are characteristic of newsletters and brochures. Throughout an entire document or in certain sections of a document, text flows (or "snakes") from the bottom of one column to the top of the next column.

To set up an entire document with snaking columns, choose the [Format] Section command. Under Columns, type the number of columns you want on the page and a measurement for the amount of space between columns and click OK. In Galley View, Word displays your text in one long, continuous column. To see your text displayed in multiple, snaking columns, choose the [Document] Page View command. To control where columns break, position the insertion point at the beginning of the text you want to move to the top of the next column and press Command-Enter to insert a section break. If you are working in Page View, the next column moves to the next page because Start: New Page is the default for new sections. Click the page forward icon to move to the next page and then position the insertion point at the top of the column. Choose the [Format] Section command, choose Start: New Column, and click OK. If you are working in Galley View, position the insertion point at the beginning of the sentence you want to move to the top of the column. Choose the [Format] Section command, choose Start: New Column, and click OK.

In some documents, you might want varying numbers of columns on the same page. Most newsletters, for instance, start with a one-column heading that spans the width of the two or more columns below it on the page. To set up varying numbers of columns on a page, position the insertion point where you want to change the number of columns (for example, after the one-column newsletter headline). Then press Command-Enter to insert a section break. Position the insertion point after the section break (move to the next page if you are working in Page View), choose the [Format] Section command, and then choose Start: No Break. Type the number of columns you want in the next section under Columns, type a measurement for the amount of space between columns, and click OK. Repeat these steps to add more sections with varying numbers of columns.

Side-by-side columns

Side-by-side columns are individual paragraphs placed next to each other to show a relationship between them. The traditional word-processing method for setting up side-by-side columns is to insert tab stops between columns. With Word 4, the easiest and most flexible way to create side-by-side columns is to create a table. A table can consist of as many rows and columns as you want. Rows, columns, and each cell of a table can be edited and formatted separately.

To create a table of side-by-side columns, position the insertion point where you want the columns and choose the [Document] Insert Table command. Type a number for Number of Columns: and a number for Number of Rows:, and click OK. When you type a number for Number of Columns, Word calculates the column width by dividing the width of the text area equally among the columns. You can type a different number for Column Width: if you want to. Word draws a grid in the text area with the number of columns and rows you specified. To type information into the table, position the insertion point in the first cell, type the text, and press Tab, Shift-Tab, and the direction keys to move from cell to cell. To type more than one paragraph in a cell, simply press the Return (or the Enter) key. Word adjusts the height of the row accordingly. You can use Word's regular character and paragraph formats to format paragraphs in a table.

See also: Formatting paragraphs, Formatting sections, Tables

Configuration file

See: Customizing Word, Word Settings (4) file

Copying formats   *Option-Command-V*

You can copy character formats or paragraph formats from one paragraph to another. To copy character formats, select a character or word that has the formats you want, press Option-Command-V, select the text you want to receive the formats, and press the Return (or the Enter) key. To copy paragaph formats, select an entire paragraph that has the formats you want, press Option-Command-V, select the paragraph you want to receive the formats, and press the Return (or the Enter) key. To copy formats as you type, press Option-Command-V first, select a paragraph that has the formats you want, and press the Return (or the Enter) key. Word pastes the formats at the insertion point, where you left off typing. To cancel copying formats, press Command-period (.) after you have pressed Option-Command-V and before you press the Return (or the Enter) key.

See also: Applying a style, Styles

Copying text   *Command-C*

You can copy text or graphics from a document to paste in another location in the same document, in a different Word document, or in a document in another application. To copy text or graphics to paste in the same or a different Word document, select the text or graphic you want to copy and choose the [Edit] Copy command. A copy of the selection is placed on the Clipboard. If necessary, open the other Word document. Then position the insertion point at the destination for the copied text or graphic and choose the [Edit] Paste command. The copied text remains on the Clipboard until you choose the [Edit] Copy command again or you choose the [Edit] Cut command.

To copy text or graphics and bypass the Clipboard, select the text or graphic, press Option-Command-C, position the insertion point where you want the copied text, and press the Return (or the Enter) key. To copy text as you type, press Option-Command-C when you reach the place to which you want to copy text, select the text to be copied, and press the Return (or the Enter) key. Word pastes the text at the insertion point.

To copy text or graphics to a document in another application, select the text or graphic in Word, choose the [Edit] Copy command, and quit Word. Start the other application, position the insertion point where you want the text, and choose the [Edit] Paste command. If you are transferring information to an application that accepts columnar data, such as a spreadsheet or database application, be sure that the data in Word is formatted with tabs or as a table so that it can be read as tabular data in the other program.

See also: Clipboard, Moving text, QuickSwitch, Selecting

Counting

To count characters, lines, paragraphs, or words in a document, choose the [Utilities] Word Count command, select the type of item you want to count, and click the Count button. In the Word Count dialog box, counts are shown for the document's Main Text, its Footnotes, and its Total. Word does not include header or footer text in the count.

To cancel a count in progress, click the Cancel button.

Cursor movement

See: Insertion point

Customizing Word

You can customize Word to better suit the way you work. With the [Edit] Commands command, you have control over more than 280 Word commands, options, and actions. You might want to add frequently used commands, options, and actions to menus and remove seldom-used commands from menus. If you're an avid keyboard user, you might want to create your own keyboard combinations for commands, options, and actions. You can also save a different configuration file that contains menu or keyboard assignments and default settings designed to fit a particular task.

Adding commands to menus

Add commands, options, and actions to menus in one of two ways, depending on the menus you want to add to: Use the Add To keyboard combination (for certain menus only) or use the [Edit] Commands command (for any menu).

Use the Add To keyboard combination Option-Command-+ (the plus sign on the keyboard) to add the following options to menus: formats, ruler icons (their word equivalents), and fonts to the Format menu; outlining options and the date and time to the Document menu; glossary entries, styles, and document names (to open the document) to the newly created Work menu. First choose the command to open the dialog box that contains the option you want to add and press Option-Command-+. Then move the bold plus-sign pointer over the dialog box option you want to add to a menu and click. To complete an addition of glossary entries, click the Cancel button to close the Glossary dialog box. To complete an addition of document names, click the Open button to close the Open dialog box. Note that to add date and time options to the Document menu, you must open the header or footer, press Option-Command-+ (the plus sign on the keyboard), and click the date or time icon.

To add any other option to a menu, choose the [Edit] Commands command and, from the list box, click the command, option, or action you want to add. Word adds this name to the upper right of the list box under Commands: If the name you chose is followed by a colon (Columns:, for example), either type more information (in our example, the number of columns) in the text box below the name or choose from the list of options. Then choose a menu to add the command to, and click either Auto, to have Word add the command to a group of related commands on that menu, or Append, to add the command to the end of the menu. Click the Add button and then click the Cancel button to close the dialog box.

To add all 280+ commands, actions, and options to menus, choose the [Edit] Commands command, press the Option key while clicking Reset, and click OK. After you click Cancel to close the Commands dialog box, you'll notice that some menus extend beyond the screen. As you drag to the bottom of the menu, Word scrolls the menu so that you can see more commands.

Removing commands from menus

To remove commands from menus, press Option-Command-hyphen (-). With the bold minus-sign pointer, choose the command you want to remove. You can also choose the [Edit] Commands command, select from the list box the name of the command you want to remove, click the Remove button, and click the Cancel button to close the dialog box.

Adding key combinations

To add a key combination to a command or an option you see on the screen, press Option-Command-+ (the plus sign on the numeric keypad), move the command-key symbol pointer over the option, and click. Type the key combination you want according to the following guidelines: Hold down any combination of the Shift, Control, Option, and Command keys and then press one other key. If the last key pressed is a character on the main keyboard, it must have been preceded by a press of the Command key. The keys on the numeric keypad and extended keyboard don't need to have shift keys assigned with them.

To add a key combination to an option or an action not found on the screen, choose the [Edit] Commands command and select the option or action from the list. Word displays the current key combination, if any, under Keys. Click the Add button and type the key combination following the guidelines above. Click the Cancel button to close the dialog box.

Comments

The [Edit] Commands command can be used both for adding commands, actions, or options to menus and for assigning key combinations.

Removing key combinations

To remove key combinations, choose the [Edit] Commands command, select from the list the command whose key combination you want to remove, select the key combination under Keys, and click the Remove button. Click the Cancel button to close the dialog box.

Saving configuration files

Command assignments, keyboard assignments, and default settings for documents are saved in a configuration file called Word Settings (4) in the System folder. When you add or remove commands or change key assignments, you modify this file unless you specify otherwise. You can create different configuration files to suit different word-processing tasks. For example, a marketing designer might use Word primarily for creating price lists and other tables. She can add options such as Merge Cells and Cell Border to menus, set the default measure to picas with the [Edit] Preferences command, set margins with the [Format] Document command, and then save these settings in a configuration file. Then, whenever the designer uses Word for creating price lists, she opens this configuration file first, and menus and other settings reflect her specifications. When the designer is simply writing a memo, however, she uses the standard Word configuration.

To save modified menus and key assignments in a different configuration file, choose the [Edit] Commands command, click the Save As button, type a name for your new configuration file, and click the Save button. Click the Cancel button to close the Commands dialog box.

Whenever you restart Word, the configuration defaults to Word Settings (4). To use your own configuration, choose the [Edit] Commands command, click the Open button, and select the name of your configuration file from the list box. Click the Open button again and click the Cancel button to close the Commands dialog box.

To restore a configuration file so that menus and keys are reset to the way they were when you last opened the file, be sure the configuration file you want to restore is open, choose the [Edit] Commands command, and click the Reset button. Note that clicking the Reset button also resets the settings you made by using the [Edit] Preferences command and resets other Word defaults you might have changed, such as automatic styles and page set-up options. To restore the original Word settings, press the Shift key while clicking the Reset button. Then click OK.

See also: Word Settings (4) file

Cut and paste

See: Moving text

Defining a style

You define a style by giving a group of character formats, paragraph formats, and ruler settings a name. By applying this style name to other paragraphs, you can quickly format them. Use either the style box on the ruler or the [Format] Define Styles command to define a style.

With the ruler

With the ruler method, you define a style by basing it on a paragraph that already has the formats you want. For instance, a heading with the formats Italic, 18 point Geneva, and Centered can be used as the basis for a style. You simply select the paragraph and name the style (*My Style*, for instance), and Word uses the paragraph's formats for the style definition. After you define the style, you can apply it to other headings in your document so that they are formatted Italic, 18 point Geneva, Centered.

To define a style with the ruler, first either select a paragraph that already has the formats you want or select a paragraph and apply the formats you want to it. (In our example, choose the [Format] Italic command and the [Font] 18 Point command and click the icon for centering on the ruler.) Then position the insertion point in the paragraph and choose the [Format] Show Ruler command to display the ruler. Click in the style box on the ruler (it displays the style name *Normal* if you haven't defined other styles), type a name for the style, and press the Return (or the Enter) key. Then click the Define button.

With the Define Styles command

Use the Define Styles method to create more than one style at a time, to base one style on another, or to link one style to another by specifying the next style that will be applied after you press the Return (or the Enter) key. To define a style with the Define Styles command, choose the [Format] Define Styles command and select New Style from the list box. In the text box, type a name for the new style. With the Define Styles dialog box still open, choose the formats you want for the style. (In our example, choose the [Format] Italic command, the [Font] 18 Point command, and click the icon for centering on the ruler.) Then click the Define button to define the style, or click the Apply button to define the style and apply it to the paragraph with the insertion point or to any selected text. The dialog box remains open so that you can define another style. To close the dialog box (and define the style and apply it to text if that hasn't already been done), click OK.

Basing one style on another

You might want to create some styles that differ from others by only one or two formats. To quickly define a style that is similar to another style, choose the [Format] Define Styles command and select New Style. Type a name for the new style and, in the Based On box, type the name of the existing style on which to base the new style. Word will include all the formatting instructions of the existing style in the new style. Then you can alter the formats by choosing commands from the Format or Font menus or by changing ruler settings. Click the Define button to define the style, or click the Apply button to define the style and apply it to selected text.

Naming styles

You can use any combination of up to 254 characters as a style name. If you usually apply styles with the keyboard combination Shift-Command-S, you might want to type both a long, descriptive name and a short name that is easier to type. For example, you might name a style both *bulleted list* and *bl*. To apply this style to a paragraph, press Shift-Command-S, type *bl*, and press the Return (or the Enter) key. To give a style both a long and a short name, choose the [Format] Define Styles command. In the Style box, type the long name, a comma, and then the short name. You can also type both a long and a short name when you define a style using the style selection box on the ruler.

See also: Applying a style, Next style, Redefining a style, Styles, Style sheets

Deleting documents

To delete a document to make more room on your disk for saving other documents, choose the [File] Delete command, choose the document to be deleted (Word displays how much disk space you will gain for each document you choose to delete), and click the Delete button. Click Yes to delete the document, or click No or Cancel if you change your mind. Note that you cannot undo this action—the document is permanently deleted from your disk.

Deleting tables and cells

To delete a cell (and the text in the cell), select the cell and choose the [Edit] Table command. Choose Selection, click either Horizontally or Vertically under Shift Cells to specify the placement of the remaining cells, and click the Delete button. To delete a row or column, position the insertion point in it and choose the [Edit] Table command. Choose Row or Column and click the Delete button. To delete an entire table (all cells and the text in them), select the table (press the Option key and double-click), choose the [Edit] Table command, and click the Delete button.

To delete only the text in a table cell and copy it to the Clipboard, select the text only (be sure the insertion point is an I-beam when selecting the text) and choose the [Edit] Cut command. If you select the entire cell by clicking anywhere on the left border of the cell, the cell format as well as the text is copied to the Clipboard when you choose the [Edit] Cut command, and the Paste command is replaced with the Paste Cells command. To delete only the text in a table cell without copying the text to the Clipboard, select the text and choose the [Edit] Clear command or press the Backspace key.

See also: Selecting, Tables

Deleting text

To delete text and copy it to the Clipboard so that you can paste it elsewhere, select the text and choose the [Edit] Cut command.

To delete text without copying it to the Clipboard, select the text and then choose the [Edit] Clear command or press the Backspace key.

Dialog boxes

A dialog box with options appears when you choose a command that is followed by an ellipsis (...). In a dialog box, boxes next to options (called *checkboxes*) indicate that you can choose more than one option from that group. (For example, in the [Format] Character dialog box, you might want to choose both Bold and All Caps.) Circles next to options (called *option buttons*) indicate that you can choose only one option from the group. (For example, you can use Superscript or Subscript, not both Superscript and Subscript.) *List boxes* (boxes within a dialog box that contain lists of options) with an arrow to the right of the box indicate that you can click the arrow to display and choose options, much as you would choose a command from a menu. When the arrow to the right of a list box is detached from the list box, you can type into the list box as well as choose from the list by clicking the arrow. *Plain text boxes* in dialog boxes provide areas for typing information (for example, the name of the document when you choose the [File] Save As command).

When you select a group of characters or paragraphs that have had different options set for them and then choose a command such as the [Format] Character command, the dialog box elements change to show that particular formats have been chosen for some of the characters. (1) Checkboxes will be gray. To give all the characters a particular format, click in the appropriate checkbox. Click again if you don't want to use the format in the selection, and click a third time to return the checkbox to gray (all characters return to their previous, different, formats). (2) Option buttons will be blank. Click one option to choose it for the entire selection. To return all the options in a group of options to their original states, click the name of the group of options (for example, click Position in the Character dialog box). (3) List boxes will be blank. Click the arrow and choose an option for the entire selection. You cannot return a list box to its original state.

To confirm your choice of dialog box options and close the dialog box, click the OK button. To cancel your choice of options and close the dialog box, click the Cancel button. Some dialog boxes have a close box in addition to or instead of a Cancel button.

Some dialog boxes contain buttons in addition to the standard OK and Cancel buttons. Clicking one of these buttons either opens a different dialog box or causes a command to be performed. The Character, Paragraph, Section, Cells, Styles, and Define Styles dialog boxes all have an Apply button. Click the Apply button to try out a format on the selected text.

If the dialog box covers text in the document that you want to see, move the dialog box out of the way by dragging its title bar to a new location on the screen.

Dividing

See: Math

Document formatting

See: Formatting documents

Editing

You can edit a document in Galley View, in Page View, or in Outline View. To insert text in any view, position the insertion point where you want the text and start typing. To insert text from the Clipboard, choose the [Edit] Paste command. Word is always in "overtype mode"—if you type while text is selected, what you type replaces the selection.

In Galley View

Select the text you want to edit and choose a command from the Edit menu, such as Cut or Copy. In Galley View, headers, footers, footnote text, and multiple columns are not displayed. To edit headers, footers, or footnotes, you must open separate windows. (For example, choose the [Document] Open Header command to display the header window and edit the header.) Text formatted for multiple columns with the [Format] Section command is displayed in one long column in Galley View. You can edit text in this column as you would any other text. To edit this text while displaying it in multiple columns, switch to Page View.

In Page View

To edit elements in their actual positions on the page, choose the [Document] Page View command. (Note that editing in Page View is somewhat slower than editing in Galley View.) Select the text you want to edit, such as text in the header (you might have to scroll to see it), and choose a command from the Edit menu, such as Cut or Copy.

In Page View, elements of the page such as headers, footers, tables, and positioned paragraphs are contained within text boundaries. To display these text boundaries as dotted lines to get a better picture of your page layout, choose the [Edit] Preferences command, check Show Text Boundaries in Page View, and click OK.

In Outline View

When you edit in Outline View, you also change the main document. For example, if you move headings to reorganize the outline, the headings and their accompanying body text will also be reorganized in Galley View.

To move text from one point to another in a long document without excessive scrolling, choose the [Document] Outlining command to switch to Outline View. Expand (display) and collapse (hide) sections by double-clicking the icon to the left of a heading until the text you want to move is displayed. Move the text above or below another heading by dragging the icon of the text you want to move. If the destination for the text is several screens away (even in Outline View), choose the [Edit] Cut command. Then scroll to the destination, position the insertion point, and choose the [Edit] Paste command.

See also: Copying text, Deleting text, Moving text, Outlining

Endnotes

See: Footnotes

Fields

See: Print merge

Finding text

See: Searching and replacing

Footer

See: Headers and footers

Footnotes

To insert a footnote (a note or reference citation) into a document, position the insertion point where you want the footnote reference mark (for example, [1]) and choose the [Document] Footnote command. Click OK to insert a number for the footnote reference mark, and type the footnote text in the footnote window. The next time you choose the [Document] Footnote command, Word inserts the next footnote reference mark in the sequence (in our example, [2]).

To edit footnote text, double-click a footnote reference mark to open the footnote window, and edit the footnote text as you would any text. To close the footnote window, double-click on the split bar.

To insert a footnote reference mark other than a number (a dagger or an asterisk, for instance), choose the [Document] Footnote command, type the symbol you want to use in the Footnote Reference Mark box, and click OK. If you continue to add footnotes with numbers as the reference marks, Word maintains the number sequence for you.

To control the placement of footnotes in the document, choose the [Format] Document command, choose from among the following options under Footnotes, and click OK:

Bottom of Page Choose to position footnotes at the bottom margin of every page that contains a footnote reference mark.

Beneath Text Choose to position a footnote directly underneath the paragraph that contains the footnote's reference mark.

End of Section: Choose to position footnotes at the end of each section or at the end of the next section for which the Include Endnotes option in the [Format] Section dialog box has been checked.

End of Document: Choose to position footnotes at the end of the entire document.

Number From: Type the number with which you want footnotes to begin if you are using the Next File button to link small documents into one large document.

Restart Each Page Choose to restart footnote numbers at 1 on each page if *Bottom of Page* or *Beneath Text* is selected. Choose to restart the numbers at 1 for each section if End of Section is selected.

Footnote reference marks are assigned the style *footnote reference*, and footnote text is assigned the style *footnote text*. These are automatic styles that are added to your style sheet the first time you use the [Document] Footnote command to insert a footnote. To format footnote reference marks or footnote text, choose the [Format] Define Styles command. Choose *footnote reference* or *footnote text* from the list box, choose commands from the Format and Font menus to redefine the style, and click OK.

To change the style of the line that separates footnotes from the main text in a printed document, choose the [Document] Footnote command, choose from the following options, and edit the separator in the window that Word displays:

Separator Click to edit the short line that separates the footnotes and the main text.

Cont. Separator Click to edit the margin-to-margin line that separates footnote text that is continued from a previous page or text column and the main text.

Cont. Notice Click to create a continuation notice for footnotes that carry over to the next page.

To delete a footnote, select the reference mark for the footnote you want to delete and choose the [Edit] Cut command. Word deletes both the reference mark and the accompanying text in the footnote window.

To view footnotes in their actual positions in the document, choose the [Document] Page View command to switch to Page View.

See also: Automatic styles, Formatting documents, Headers and footers, Page View

Fonts

See: Formatting characters

Formatting

Formatting controls the appearance of your document. Bold and italic characters, indented paragraphs, the number of columns on a page, and the margins for your entire document are all examples of formatting. Four commands on the Format menu—Character, Paragraph,

Section, and Document—control formatting, from the smallest element of a document (an individual character) to the largest (the entire document).

Character formats

Character formats affect individual characters. For example, you can format only one letter in a word in bold (BlackStone), or you can format all the characters in a word in bold (**BlackStone**). Letters, numbers, symbols, spaces, and tabs are all considered to be characters and can be formatted. For example, to create a short line, press the Spacebar a few times and select the spaces. (To display the selected spaces as small dots, choose the [Edit] Show ¶ command.) Then choose the [Format] Underline command. Other aspects of character formats are font and font size, superscript, subscript, color, and spacing between characters.

Paragraph formats

Paragraph formats affect individual paragraphs. For example, the first two paragraphs of your document might be aligned flush left with the margin and the rest of the paragraphs might be indented ½ inch from the margin. Other aspects of paragraph formats are changes to the ruler (such as tab stops), spacing above and below a paragraph, and borders.

Section formats

Section formats affect individual sections. For example, your document might consist of two sections—the first with only one column and the other with three columns. You create sections by pressing Command-Enter at the place in the document where you want a new section to begin. The [Format] Section command enables you to specify the number of columns, the position of the new section, line numbers, page numbers, and headers and footers.

Document formats

Document formats affect an entire document. For example, you can set the top, bottom, left, and right margins for the whole document. Other aspects of document formatting are setting up facing pages, choosing footnote position, and setting default tab stops.

Formatting and styles

To speed up applying character and paragraph formats, you can group the formats together and give them a name—a style name. All text has the default style *Normal*, which you can change just as you would any other style. You can add other formatting to text in addition to the formatting included in the style. To delete formatting you've added to text so that the text conforms to its original style, select the text and press Shift-Command-Spacebar, or choose the [Format] Plain For Style command.

See also: Formatting characters, Formatting documents, Formatting paragraphs, Formatting sections, Styles

---

Formatting characters   *Command-D*

To format individual characters, select the character(s), choose a font and font size from the Font menu, and choose Plain Text, Bold, Italic, Underline, Outline, or Shadow from the Format menu. To choose from among all character formats, choose the [Format] Character command, choose one or more of the options listed below, click the Apply button if you want to try out the formats, and when you find the formats you like, click OK. To change formats while typing new text, position the insertion point where you want to begin the new format and then perform the steps above without selecting any text.

Font: Choose a font (typeface) from the alphabetic list of the fonts included in your Macintosh System folder.

Size: Choose a font size from the list or type one. If you type a size that is not on the list, Word scales one of the available sizes to fit, so the characters might look ragged.

Underline: Choose None to turn off all underlining, Single to underline words and spaces with a single line, Word to underline only words (excluding spaces) with a single line, Double to underline all words and spaces with a double line, or Dotted to underline all words and spaces with a dotted line.

Color: Choose a color for the current font. If your Macintosh does not display color, you might still be able to print in color, depending on your printer.

Style Choose Bold, Italic, Outline, Shadow, or Strikethrough to apply those styles to the characters. Choose Small Caps to convert lowercase letters to uppercase letters in the next smaller font size. Choose All Caps to convert lowercase letters to uppercase letters in the same font size. Choose Hidden to give text the hidden text format. Hidden text is displayed with a dotted underline if the Show Hidden Text option is checked in the [Edit] Preferences dialog box; otherwise, the text is hidden.

Position Choose Normal to position text on the baseline, Superscript to position text above the baseline, or Subscript to position text below the baseline. In the By: box, type the number of points you want above or below the baseline for Superscript or Subscript.

Spacing Choose Normal for normal spacing between characters, Condensed to decrease the spacing between characters, or Expanded to increase the spacing between characters. In the By: box, type the number of points by which you want to condense or expand the spacing between characters. (In typesetting terminology, spacing between letters is referred to as *kerning*.)

To delete from text all character formats except the font and font size or to stop using the formats you chose while typing text, select the text and choose the [Format] Plain Text command.

Formatting documents

To set formats for the entire document, choose the [Format] Document command, choose from the following options, and click OK:

Margins: Type measurements for the top, bottom, left, and right margins. If you have headers or footers that are too large for the margins, Word increases the margin size. If you don't want Word to increase the margin size, type a minus sign in front of the length for that margin. (For example, type −.25 to ensure that the margin remains 0.25 inch). Then, if the header or footer doesn't fit, Word prints the text in the footer overlapping the text in the text area. (Note that the Apple LaserWriter requires minimum margins of $\frac{1}{2}$ inch.)

Mirror Even/Odd Margins Check this option to set up facing pages for back-to-back copying.

Even/Odd Headers Check this option to add Open Odd Header/Footer and Open Even Header/Footer commands to the Document menu if you want headers and footers to differ on even and odd pages.

Widow Control Check this option to ensure that there will be no single line (widow) at the top of a page after pagination. Uncheck this option if you want to print as many lines on a page as possible.

Gutter: Type a measurement to use as extra space at the left margin of odd pages and the right margin of even pages. This measurement allows space for binding double-sided documents.

Number Pages From: Type the starting page number for the document. If the document is one of a series of linked documents and you want the page numbering to continue from the last page of the preceding document, type *0* (zero). (Type *1* as the starting page number if the document is the first in the series.)

Number Lines From: Type the line number of the first line in the document.

Default Tab Stops: Type a measurement for the default tab stops for the entire document. On the ruler, tiny horizontal lines mark the default tab stops.

Footnotes Position: Choose Bottom of Page to position footnotes at the bottom margin. Choose Beneath Text to position footnotes directly underneath the paragraph that contains the footnote reference mark. Choose End of Section to position footnotes at the end of each section or at the end of the next section. You should then check the Include Endnotes option in the [Format] Section dialog box. Choose End of Document to position footnotes at the end of the entire document.

Footnotes Number From: Type the number with which you want the footnote reference marks to start.

Footnotes Restart Each Page Choose this option to restart footnote numbers at 1 on each page if Bottom of Page or Beneath Text is selected. Check this option to restart the numbers at 1 for each section if End of Section is selected.

Next File Choose this option to open the Open File dialog box in order to link a series of files to create one document.

To save the settings in the [Format] Document dialog box as the default settings for new documents you create, click the Set Default button and then click OK.

See also: Footnotes, Linking documents, Margins, Numbering lines, Page numbers

Formatting paragraphs   *Command-M*

To set formats for an individual paragraph, select the paragraph, choose the [Format] Paragraph command, and choose from the options described below. Click the Apply button if you want to try out the formats, and when you find the ones you like, click OK. When you choose the [Format] Paragraph command, the ruler is displayed, along which you can move indent markers; you can see the corresponding measurements in the Paragraph dialog box. You can use the ruler to set other paragraph formats as well.

Indents Type measurements to indicate how far to indent a paragraph from the left and right margins and to indicate how far to indent only the first line of the paragraph from the left margin.

Spacing For Line:, type a measurement to specify line spacing for a paragraph. (Line spacing, or leading, is the distance from the bottom of one line to the bottom of the next line within the paragraph.) Word adjusts the line spacing measurement if the measurement you type causes lines to overlap. If you want lines to overlap, type a minus sign in front of the number you want. For Before:, type a measurement to specify the amount of space you want above the entire paragraph. For After:, type a measurement to specify the amount of space you want below the entire paragraph. For any of the Spacing options, you can type the number of lines by typing the abbreviation *li* after the measurement. (One line = 12 points of vertical space.) For example, typing *2 li* results in a double-spaced paragraph.

Page Break Before Check this option to ensure that when Word repaginates, it will place a page break before the paragraph. Give this format, for example, to a major heading that should start on a new page.

Keep With Next ¶ Check this option to keep a paragraph and the following paragraph together when Word repaginates. Give this format, for example, to a graphic and its caption to ensure that the two are always on the same page.

Line Numbering Check this option to turn line numbering on, or uncheck this option to turn line numbering off, for a particular paragraph. This option is available only if you've chosen the [Format] Section command and checked Line Numbers.

Keep Lines Together Check this option to keep all lines within a paragraph together when Word repaginates.

You can click the Tab button to set tabs, the Borders button to give a paragraph borders, and the Position button to position the paragraph on the page.

See also: Borders, Numbering lines, Positioning paragraphs, Ruler, Tabs

Formatting sections

To format a section of a document, be sure the insertion point is in the section you want to format (above the section break you've inserted with Command-Enter) and choose the [Format] Section command. Choose from the following options, click the Apply button if you want to try out the formats, and then click OK when you're satisfied.

Start: Choose New Page to start a section on a new page, New Column to start the section at the top of the next column, No Break to continue the section on the same page as the previous section, Even Page to start the section on the next even-numbered page, or Odd Page to start the section on the next odd-numbered page. If necessary, Word adds a blank page when you choose Even Page or Odd Page.

Include Endnotes Check this option to include footnotes at the end of the section. You can choose this option only when you've set the footnote position to End of Section by using the [Format] Document command.

Page Number Check Auto to have Word add page numbers to a section continuing in sequence from a previous section. Check Restart at 1 to restart numbering the pages at 1 in the section. Choose a format for the page number: 1 2 3 for Arabic numerals, I II III for uppercase Roman numerals, i ii iii for lowercase Roman numerals, A B C for uppercase letters, or a b c for lowercase letters. For From Top:, type the distance you want from the top of the page to the top of the page number. For From Right:, type the distance you want from the right edge of the page to the left side of the page number. You can specify From Top: and From Right: only if you have chosen Auto page numbering.

Line Numbers Choose Off if you don't want to number lines, By Page to start line numbering at 1 on each page, By Section to start at 1 for a section, or Continuous to continue numbering in order from the last number in the previous section. For Count By:, type a number by which you want to increment line numbers. For From Text:, type a measurement for the distance from the left margin to the right edge of the line number.

Columns Type a number for the number of columns in the section. For Spacing:, type a measurement for the distance between columns. Default spacing is 0.5 inch.

Header/Footer For From Top:, type a distance from the top of the page to the top of the header. For From Bottom:, type a distance from the bottom of the page to the bottom of the footer. Check First Page Special if you don't want the first page of the section to have a header, footer, or page number, or if you want a different header or footer for the first page of the section. Checking this option adds the commands Open First Header and Open First Footer to the Document menu so that you can create the special header or footer.

To save the settings in the [Format] Section dialog box as the default settings for new documents you create, click the Set Default button and then click OK.

Comments

Section formats for subsequent sections are the same as for the preceding section unless you change them.

See also: Columns, Footnotes, Headers and footers, Numbering lines, Page numbers

Form letters

See: Print merge

Formulas

To add mathematical symbols such as radical signs and fractions and other symbols such as large brackets to formulas, you type special typesetting codes with the [Edit] Show ¶ command on. When you choose the [Edit] Hide ¶ command, Word displays the formula in its final format. Some examples of the symbols you can produce are shown on the following page.

$\sqrt{225}$

$\dfrac{1}{100}$

| My |
| Oh |
| ▪ My ▪ |

To enter a formula, first be sure that the Symbol font is installed on your System disk. Then choose the [Edit] Show ¶ command if necessary, press Command-Option-\ (backslash) to insert the formula character (.\), and type one of the typesetting commands listed below (either uppercase or lowercase is acceptable). Choose any options (preceded by Command-Option-\), and type the arguments, enclosing them in parentheses.

Do not insert spaces between the typesetting command, options, and arguments, and be sure to use the correct number of parentheses. If you introduce an error into a formula, Word will not display the final format when you choose the [Edit] Hide ¶ command.

.\A (Array)

Draws a two-dimensional array. When there is more than one column, arguments are displayed in order by rows. The options are

.\AL	Aligns arguments left within columns
.\AR	Aligns arguments right within columns
.\AC	Centers arguments within columns
.\CO$n$	Sets the number of columns to n
.\VS$n$	Sets vertical spacing between columns to n points
.\HS$n$	Sets horizontal spacing between columns to n points

Example

Formula:

\A\AC\CO3(1,2,3,4,5,6)

Result:

123
456

.\B (Bracket)

Draws around arguments the bracket you specify. The size of the bracket corresponds to the argument's size. The options are

.\LC.\c   Draws the bracket (*c*) on the left side of the argument

.\RC.\c   Draws the bracket (*c*) on the right side of the argument

.\BC.\c   Draws the bracket (*c*) on both sides of the argument

You can specify any character to be used as the bracket. If you type the opening bracket {, [, (, or < for the .\BC option, Word places the corresponding closing bracket on the right side of the argument.

Example

Formula:

\B\BC\|(-12).=.12

Result:

|-12| = 12

.\D (Displace)

Inserts space, draws a horizontal line, or does both between two characters. The options are

.\FO*n*   Adds space to the right (forward) by *n* points

.\BA*n*   Adds space to the left (backward) by *n* points

.\LI   Draws a line between two characters

Note that you must type parentheses after the options—even though the Displace formula doesn't take any arguments.

Examples

Formula:

F\D\FO35()A\D\FO35()R

Result:

F   A   R

Formula:

F\D\FO35\LI()A\D\FO35\LI()R

Result:

F___A___R

.\F (Fraction)

Draws a fraction with the numerator centered above the line and the denominator centered below the line. There are no options for this command. Arguments can be numbers, letters, symbols, or other formulas.

Example

Formula:

\F(1,(15-x))

Result:

$$\frac{1}{(15-x)}$$

.\I (Integral)

Draws an integral equation from three arguments—the lower limit, the upper limit, and the integrand. Some options allow you to specify the use of symbols other than the integral symbol. The options are

.\SU	Changes the symbol to the summation symbol, a capital sigma (Σ)
.\PR	Changes the symbol to the product symbol, a capital pi (Π)
.\IN	Changes the format of the integral symbol so that the limits are placed to the right of the symbol instead of above and below
.\FC.\c	Changes the symbol to the character c at a fixed height
.\VC.\c	Changes the symbol to the character c at a variable height matching the height of the integrand

Example

Formula:

\I\IN(a,b,f)

Result:

$$\int_a^b f$$

.\L (List)

Draws a list of arguments separated by commas. (The only other way to include commas in the final formula is to type the Command-Option-\ (backslash) character before each comma.)

Example

Formula:

\F(\L(400.miles,.2.kilometers),.\L(8.hours,.15.minutes))

Result:

<u>400 miles, 2 kilometers</u>
   8 hours, 15 minutes

.\O (Overstrike)

Draws successive arguments on top of one another. The options are

.\AL	Aligns characters at the left edge
.\AR	Aligns characters at the right edge
.\AC	Centers characters over one another (default)

Example

Formula:

x.\O(=,/).y

Result:

x ≠ y

.\R (Radical)

Draws a radical symbol. If you give one argument, it appears under the radical; if you give two, the first argument appears over the radical and the second appears under the radical.

Example

Formula:

`\R(5,32).=.2`

Result:

$$\sqrt[5]{32} = 2$$

.\S (Superscript or Subscript)

Draws arguments above (superscript) or below (subscript) the baseline. The options are

.\UP*n*	Moves the argument up *n* points from the baseline
.\DO*n*	Moves the argument down *n* points from the baseline
.\AI*n*	Adds *n* points above the ascender of the argument
.\DI*n*	Adds *n* points below the descender of the argument

Example

Formula:

`area.=.πr\S\UP4(2)`

Result:

$$area = πr^2$$

.\X (Box)

Draws a box around one argument. The options are

.\BO	Draws the bottom box border
.\LE	Draws the left box border
.\RI	Draws the right box border
.\TO	Draws the top box border

Without options, Word draws the entire box.

Example

Formula:

\X(Box.me)

Result:

Box me

To move formulas to another application, convert the final formula into a graphic. First, be sure that [Edit] Hide ¶ is on; then select the formula and press Command-Option-D. Word copies the formula as a picture to the Clipboard. Quit Word, start the other application, position the insertion point where you want the graphic, and choose the application's [Edit] Paste command.

Full menus

When you first start Word, it displays Short menus: menus that contain commands for basic word-processing tasks. Full menus contain additional commands for more advanced word-processing tasks. To switch to Full menus, choose the [Edit] Full Menus command. The command name changes to [Edit] Short Menus. To switch back to Short menus, choose the command again.

Comments

This reference guide assumes that you are using Full menus.

Galley View

Galley View is Word's default document view, which displays text without the following formatting: page numbers, headers, footers, footnotes, and multiple text columns. In Galley View, headers, footers, and footnotes are in separate windows. Text you've arranged in multiple columns by setting options in the [Format] Section command is displayed in one long column. Because Word doesn't display all formatting, typing and editing are faster in Galley View than in Page View. To take advantage of the faster typing and editing, create your documents in Galley View and then alternate between Page View and Print Preview to lay out the page(s) and to finalize formatting.

See also: Formatting, Formatting sections, Page View, Print Preview

---

Glossary   *Command-Backspace*

A glossary in Word is a storage area for frequently used text or graphics (also called a *boilerplate*). By including the text or graphic in the glossary and giving it a name, you can insert it anywhere in a document by pressing Command-Backspace, typing the name, and pressing the Return (or the Enter) key. Each graphic or piece of text you store in a glossary is called a *glossary entry*. When you choose the [Edit] Glossary command, Word displays the Standard Glossary, which includes entries you can use to insert the current date and time and the print merge characters (« and ») into your document. You can add glossary entries to the Standard Glossary, which means they will be available anytime you use Word, or you can create a separate glossary for use with special documents. For example, you might create a glossary called "Slogans" that contains slogans you use whenever you're creating an advertisement or a brochure for your company.

To add a glossary entry to the Standard Glossary, type the text or paste the graphic, select the text or graphic, and choose the [Edit] Glossary command. Type an easy-to-remember name in the Name box, and click the Define button. Word inserts the name of the new glossary entry in the list box and a portion of the entry at the bottom of the dialog box. If the glossary entry contains a graphic, when you select the glossary entry name a small box appears at the bottom of the dialog box. Click the close box or the Cancel button to close the Glossary dialog box.

To create a glossary separate from Word's Standard Glossary, choose the [Edit] Glossary command and then choose the [File] New command. Click Yes if you would like to clear any nonstandard glossary entries that you've added, and follow the steps above for adding glossary entries. (You'll name and save the separate glossary when you quit.)

To insert a glossary entry from the Standard Glossary into your document, position the insertion point where you want the text or graphic to appear, press Command-Backspace, type the name of the glossary entry, and press the Return (or the Enter) key. If you forget the names for your glossary entries, choose the [Edit] Glossary command, select the entry you want from the list, and click the Insert button.

To insert a glossary entry from a separate glossary you've created, choose the [Edit] Glossary command and the [File] New command. Click Yes to clear all the glossary entries, choose the [File] Open command, double-click the name of the glossary you want to use, and click the close box. To insert an entry, press Command-Backspace, type the entry's name, and press the Return (or the Enter) key.

To delete a glossary entry, choose the [Edit] Glossary command and select from the list box the entry you want to delete. Choose the [Edit] Cut command and choose Yes when Word asks if you want to delete the entry. Then click the close box.

To rename a glossary entry, choose the [Edit] Glossary command and select from the list box the entry you want to rename. Type a new name in the Name box, click the Define button, and click the close box.

To print the contents of the glossary, choose the [Edit] Glossary command and then choose the [File] Print command.

When you quit, Word asks if you want to save the glossary. If you click Yes, Word displays the Save As dialog box. If you added entries to the Standard Glossary, Word proposes ''Standard Glossary'' as the glossary's name. If you created a separate glossary, type a name for the glossary. Then click the Save button. If you made changes to the Standard Glossary and then saved it under a different name, the next time you start up Word, a new Standard Glossary will be formed. You can access the glossary you modified by opening it—choose [Edit] Glossary and then [File] Open.

Graphics

To paste a graphic into a Word document, copy the graphic from a Macintosh graphics program to the Clipboard and quit the graphics program. Start Word or use MultiFinder and QuickSwitch to shift to Word, position the insertion point in the document where you want the graphic to appear, and choose the [Edit] Paste command.

To place an empty frame that reserves space for a graphic or for drawing a graphic with PostScript commands, position the insertion point where you want the frame and choose the [Document] Insert Graphics command. To see the graphics frame, choose the [Edit] Show ¶ command. To draw an outline around the frame, click to the left of the frame to select it and choose [Format] Outline. Because graphics and graphic frames are characters, you can add any character formatting such as Outline, Bold, or Shadow to them.

To resize the frame for the graphic, click inside the frame to select it and drag the graphic handles (small black boxes) until the space for the graphic is the size you want. To size and scale the graphic (the graphic will conform to the frame's size), select the graphic (and its frame), hold down the Shift key, and drag the graphic handles. To shrink the frame to the smallest size that will hold the graphic, select the frame and double-click.

To speed up scrolling in a document that contains graphics, choose the [Edit] Preferences command, check Use Picture Placeholders, and click OK. Word inserts gray rectangles in place of the graphics in Galley View, Outline View, and Page View. When you choose the [File] Print Preview command or print the document, Word displays or prints the graphics.

To convert text—such as the final form of a Word formula—into a graphic, select the text and press Command-Option-D. Word copies the text to the Clipboard as a graphic. Position the insertion point where you want the graphic and choose the [Edit] Paste command.

To superimpose text onto a graphic, position the insertion point to the right of the graphic and press Return. Then type immediately after the graphic the text you want to superimpose, and select both the graphic and the text. Choose the [Format] Position command, select from the options to position the text and the graphic in the same place on the page, and click OK. Word inserts paragraph property marks (small black squares) to the left of the graphic and text. Next, insert a normal paragraph between the graphic and the text by clicking at the right edge of the graphic, pressing Return, and pressing Command-Shift-P. The paragraph property mark for this paragraph disappears.

To check the position of the text and graphic on the page, choose the [File] Print Preview command. In some cases, even in Print Preview, the graphic will overlap the text and you will have to print to see the result. To position the text horizontally within the graphic, change the left indent of the paragraph that contains the text. To position the text vertically within the graphic, select the paragraph of text, choose the [Format] Paragraph command, and type a number for Spacing Before or Spacing After.

See also: MultiFinder, Positioning paragraphs, QuickSwitch

Gutter margin

See: Margins

Headers and footers

To insert a header or footer into a document, choose the [Document] Open Header or Open Footer command, type the text for the header or footer (chapter name and number, for instance), and, if you want, click the icons to insert the page number, current date, and current time:

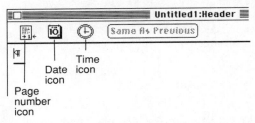

Then format the text by choosing commands from the Format menu and by using the ruler (the [Edit] Show Ruler command), and click the close box. Word inserts the same header or footer at the top or bottom, respectively, of each page in all sections of the document.

To insert different headers or footers into different sections of your document, position the insertion point in the section that is to have its own header or footer. Choose the [Document] Open Header or Open Footer command and edit the original header or footer. The headers (or footers) of sections found between the one you just created and the next specifically created header (or footer) will change to match the new one. If no other headers (or footers) have been specified, the headers (or footers) of the rest of the document will be changed. If you edit a header or footer for a different section and then decide to use the previous section's header or footer, click the Same As Previous button.

To create a special header or footer for a title page, press Command-Enter to insert a section break where you want the title page to end, position the insertion point above that section break, and choose the

[Format] Section command. Select First Page Special and click OK. Then choose the [Document] Open First Header or Open First Footer command, create the header or footer for the first page, and click the close box.

To create different headers or footers for even-numbered and odd-numbered pages, choose the [Format] Document command. Check the Even/Odd Headers option (and Mirror Even/Odd Margins if you want inside and outside margins of even-numbered and odd-numbered pages to be the same) and click OK. Then choose the [Document] Open Even Header or Footer command to create the header or footer for even-numbered pages, and choose the [Document] Open Odd Header or Footer command to create the header or footer for odd-numbered pages.

Word assigns headers the style *header* and footers the style *footer*. These automatic styles are added to your style sheet the first time you use the [Document] Open Header or Open Footer command. To format the headers or footers differently, choose the [Format] Define Styles command and then choose *header* or *footer* from the list box. Choose formatting options from the Format and Font menus to change the header or footer style definition, and click OK.

Word reserves space at the top and bottom of the page for the header and footer and makes adjustments if the header or footer won't fit in the specified margin. Sometimes, you might want the header or footer to overlap the main text area. (For example, you might want a header in the left margin.) To ensure that Word doesn't adjust spacing to keep the header within the margin, choose the [Format] Section command and type a negative number for From Top: (for headers) or for From Bottom: (for footers). Then click OK.

In Page View, headers and footers are displayed in their exact positions on the page, not in separate windows. To create or edit a header or footer in Page View, choose the [Document] Open Header or Open Footer command. Word scrolls the page to the position of the header or footer and positions the insertion point in the header or footer.

To move headers or footers up or down, choose the [File] Print Preview command. Click the margins icon and drag the header or footer up or down. To drag the header or footer into the main text area, hold down the Shift key as you drag. If you want to type exact measurements for header or footer placement, position the insertion point in the section and choose the [Format] Section command. In the Header/Footer box, type the measurements in the From Top: and From Bottom: boxes and click OK.

See also: Automatic styles, Defining a style, Footnotes, Margins

Help

To get on-screen information about Word, choose the [Window] Help command and choose a topic from the alphabetic list of topics by double-clicking the one you want. Word displays information about that topic.

To get information on a specific command, press Command-?. Use the question mark pointer to choose a command for which you need help. Word then displays information about that command. If you press Command-? when a dialog box is open, Word displays information about that dialog box.

The buttons in the Help window provide control over which screens of Help are displayed.

Topics Displays the alphabetic list of Help topics

Cancel Closes the Help window and returns you to your document

Previous Displays the previous Help topic

Next Displays the next Help topic

The Help window also displays the page number in *Reference to Microsoft Word* where you can find more information about the topic you've chosen.

Comments
When you choose the [Window] Help command or press Command-?, Word asks you to locate the document Word Help if it is not on one of the current disks or in the current folder. To locate Word Help, click the Drive button to see documents on another disk or click the Eject button to eject a disk and insert a different disk. After you locate Word Help on a disk, double-click Word Help in the list box. Word displays the Help window.

See also: Installing Word, Product support

Hidden text

Hidden text is a character format you assign to text or graphics you don't want to be displayed or printed. As you write a term paper, for example, you might want to include notes about the reference sources you're using. You can type the notes, format them as hidden text, and then display or print the notes only when you need them. When Word displays hidden text, the text has a dotted underline.

To format text as hidden, select the text, choose the [Format] Character command, check Hidden, and click OK. To display hidden text, choose the [Edit] Preferences command, check Show Hidden Text, and click OK. To print hidden text, choose the [File] Print command, check Print Hidden Text, and click OK. Word then prints all hidden text in the document regardless of whether you've chosen to display it.

You can use hidden text formatting for the index and table of contents entries, PostScript commands, and QuickSwitch characters in your document. When you use the [Document] Insert Index Entry or Insert TOC Entry commands, Word assigns the hidden text format to the index or table of contents codes.

Comments

To ensure that your page breaks and line breaks will be accurate, do not display hidden text when you paginate or hyphenate your document. Choose the [Edit] Preferences command, click Show Hidden Text to remove the check, and click OK.

See also: Indexing, PostScript, QuickSwitch, Table of contents

Hyphenating

Word offers three types of hyphens: normal hyphens, optional hyphens, and nonbreaking hyphens.

Normal hyphens (-)

To insert normal hyphens in a document, simply press the hyphen key (-). Insert a normal hyphen in a compound word in which the hyphen is part of the spelling—*ex-president*, for example. In some documents, inserting normal hyphens as you type will be the only "hyphenating" you'll have to do.

Optional hyphens (Command--)

In some documents, particularly in those with justified text or text in columns, you'll want to have Word add optional hyphens. Choose the [Utilities] Hyphenate command. Word then fills each line with as much text as possible by moving syllables to the ends of previous lines and adding the optional hyphens. You can also insert an optional hyphen manually by pressing Command-hyphen (-).

To remove all the optional hyphens in a document (important if you've edited your document since you last hyphenated and want to rehyphenate later), choose the [Utilities] Change command, type ^– (caret, hyphen) in the Find What: box, leave the Change To: box blank, and click Change All.

If you choose the [Utilities] Hyphenate command to insert optional hyphens, several choices are available.

Hyphenate All To hyphenate your entire document, position the insertion point at the beginning of your document, choose the [Utilities] Hyphenate command, and click Hyphenate All.

Hyphenate Selection To hyphenate selected words or paragraphs, select the text, choose the [Utilities] Hyphenate command, and click Hyphenate Selection.

Start Hyphenation (select individually) To control Word's hyphenation of your text, choose the [Utilities] Hyphenate command and click the Start Hyphenation button. In the Hyphenate box, Word displays the first word to be hyphenated broken into syllables with its proposed hyphen selected. If the hyphen is where you want it, click Change to hyphenate the word and display the next hyphenated word. If you want to change the placement of the hyphen, click on another hyphen or between two letters and then click Change. A vertical line shows you where the margin would be in relation to the word break. If you want to leave the word unhyphenated, click No Change. Continue to hyphenate by clicking the Start Hyphenation button again and following the steps above.

Hyphenate Capitalized Words To enable hyphenation of words that begin with capital letters, click the Hyphenate Capitalized Words option.

Nonbreaking hyphens (Command-~)

If your document contains words you don't want to be broken between two lines (''off-off-Broadway,'' for example), you can insert a nonbreaking hyphen by pressing Command-~ (tilde). Words you've given nonbreaking hyphens will not break when you use the Hyphenate command.

Comments

Because hyphenating affects line breaks and, ultimately, page breaks, you should hyphenate just before printing a document. If you are working with a multiple-column layout such as a newsletter's, however, where hyphenating can determine how much text goes in each column, you'll want to hyphenate before you decide where the beginning of the next column will be.

ImageWriter

See: Printers

Inches

See: Measurements

Indenting

See: Formatting paragraphs

Indexing

To create an index for your document, you insert index entry codes in the document and then compile the index.

Inserting codes

To insert index codes for text already in your document, select the text and choose the [Document] Insert Index Entry command. Word inserts a .i. code before the text and a ; (semicolon) code after the text. If the word to be indexed falls at the end of a paragraph or before an end-of-line mark, Word omits the semicolon. Word formats the index codes—but not the text—as hidden text.

To insert codes for text that will appear in your index but not in your document, position the insertion point where you want the entry and choose the [Document] Insert Index Entry command. Word formats the index codes as hidden text, leaving the insertion point between the codes so that you can type the text for the index. When you type text between the index entry codes, Word formats the text as hidden so that it will not be included as part of your main document.

The following phrase shows both kinds of coded index entries—text that is part of the document and text that isn't:

```
To ensure that the .i.wallpaper pattern;
is aligned.i.aligning patterns; at the corners...
```

To hide the index codes and accompanying text that won't appear in the document, choose the [Edit] Preferences command, click Show Hidden Text, and click OK. The hidden text is no longer displayed:

```
To ensure that the wallpaper pattern
is aligned at the corners...
```

Most indexes have more than one entry level. For example, "wallpaper patterns" might be a main level entry and "aligning" might be a subentry under "wallpaper patterns." To code this relationship, you type a colon between the main entry and the subentry:

```
.i.wallpaper patterns:aligning;
```

To add a second subentry, "choosing," type the following:

```
.i.wallpaper patterns:choosing;
```

The compiled index would look like this:

```
wallpaper patterns
   aligning 28
   choosing 19
```

When you compile the index, you can choose to have subentries indented under main entries (as shown) or separated by semicolons (;) on the same line as the main entries. See "Compiling the index" in this section.

Codes for formatting and page ranges

By inserting additional codes between the .i. and ; codes, you can add formatting and page ranges to the compiled index.

To format the index with bold or italic page numbers, insert the letter *B* or *I* to the right of the i in the .i. code:

.iB.wallpaper;

To include a cross reference or any text in place of the page number in the index, insert to the left of the semicolon a pound sign (#) and the text:

.i.wallpaper designs#(See wallpaper patterns);

To have an entry show a range of page numbers for a topic that continues over several pages, insert a left parenthesis (symbol to the right of the i in the .i. code on the page on which the topic starts,

.i(.wallpaper patterns:aligning;

and insert a right parenthesis) symbol to the right of the i in the .i. code on the page on which the topic ends:

.i).wallpaper patterns:aligning;

Compiling the index

After inserting index entry codes in your document, compile the index by choosing the [Utilities] Index command, setting the following options, and clicking Start.

Format: Choose Nested to indent subentries under main entries. Choose Run-in to place subentries separated by semicolons on the same lines as their main entries.

Index Characters: To compile the entire index for a small document, choose All. For a larger document, compile the index section-by-section by typing a range of letters of the alphabet in the From: and To: boxes. For example, type *a* in the From: box and *m* in the To: box to compile index entries within that range of letters only. Then compile from *n* to *z*.

Word compiles and alphabetizes the index entries, inserts page numbers, and places the index at the end of your document, with a section mark before it to separate the index from your main document. When you choose to index a document by specifying several different ranges with From: and To:, Word inserts section marks between sections of the index. If you want to, you can delete the section marks.

See also: Hidden text, Selecting, Linking documents

Inserting text

To insert text into a document by typing, position the insertion point where you want the text and then type.

To insert text from the Clipboard, position the insertion point where you want the text and choose the [Edit] Paste command.

To insert text from the Glossary, press Command-Backspace, type the glossary name, and press the Return (or the Enter) key. If you don't remember the glossary name, choose the [Edit] Glossary command and double-click the name in the list box.

See also: Clipboard, Copying text, Glossary, Insertion point

Insertion point

The insertion point is the blinking vertical line that indicates where text is to be inserted when you type or paste from the Clipboard or Glossary. To position the insertion point, move the mouse pointer to the area in which you want to insert text, and then click. Note that the mouse pointer is in the shape of an I-beam when it is in the text window.

See also: Deleting text, Inserting text

Installing Word

Before installing Word 4, make copies of the Word Program disk, and the Utilities 1 and Utilities 2 disks. That way, if anything happens to your master disks, you have backup copies.

Word 4 does not include the System or the Finder, so be sure you have copies of the most current versions for your Macintosh.

On two 800 KB drives

First format two disks—a System disk and a Word disk. Copy these files onto the System disk: System, Finder, Keyboard, Mouse, Printer Driver, and Clipboard. (This disk will also have extra space for storing documents you create with Word.) Copy these files onto the Word disk: Microsoft Word, Standard Glossary, MS Dictionary, Word Help, and Word Hyphenation.

You can tailor the Word disk to meet your needs. For example, if you rarely hyphenate in your documents, don't copy the Word Hyphenation file onto the program disk; likewise, if you rarely use the on-line Help feature, don't copy the Word Help file. When you use Hyphenation or Help, Word will ask you to locate the appropriate file by inserting in a drive the disk that contains the file.

To install Word 4, insert your System disk in the internal drive and your Word disk in the external (or second internal) drive. To start Word 4, double-click the Microsoft Word program icon.

On a hard disk

You probably already have on your hard disk a System folder that contains files such as System, Finder, Keyboard, Mouse, Printer Driver, and Clipboard. Create a Word 4 folder on your hard disk and into this folder copy the following files: Microsoft Word, Standard Glossary, MS Dictionary, Word Help, and Word Hyphenation.

To start Word 4, open the Word 4 folder and double-click the Microsoft Word program icon.

See also: Printers, Starting Word

Italic

See: Formatting characters

Justifying text

See: Aligning paragraphs

Kerning

See: Formatting characters

Labels

See: Mailing labels

LaserWriter

See: Printers

Line breaks   *Shift-Return*

To start a new line without starting a new paragraph, hold down the
Shift key and press Return. Word inserts a new line character—a left-
facing arrow. To see the newline character, choose the [Edit] Show ¶
command.

You can also control line breaks by hyphenating words throughout
your document.

See also: Hyphenating, Paragraph mark

Line drawing

See: Borders

Line spacing

See: Formatting paragraphs

Linking documents

It's a good idea to break a long document (hundreds of pages) into smaller documents. By linking these smaller documents, you can still create one table of contents and one index and paginate and print all the documents sequentially.

To link several documents, open the first document in the series, choose the [Format] Document command, and click the Next File button. Double-click the name of the next document from the list and click OK. Then open the second document and follow the same procedure. Do this for all subsequent documents in the series. After you choose the next file, the Next File button changes to Reset Next File so that you can cancel the link between documents if you want to.

After linking, you can compile a complete table of contents and index and sequentially number pages, footnotes, lines, and paragraphs throughout all the documents.

Table of contents and index

To compile one table of contents for all documents, first follow the procedures above for linking the documents. Then open the first document in the series, choose the [Utilities] Table of Contents command, choose from among the options, and click OK. Word compiles the entries for the table of contents from all the linked documents and places the table of contents at the beginning of the first document in the series.

To compile one index for all documents, first follow the procedures above for linking the documents. Then open the first document in the series, choose the [Utilities] Index command, choose from among the options, and click OK. Word compiles the index entries from all the linked documents and places the index at the end of the last document in the series.

Sequential page numbers

Open the first document in the series and select the entire document. Then choose the [Format] Section command, check Auto under Page Number, and click OK. Next, choose the [Format] Document command, type *1* in the Number Pages From: box, and click OK. For all other documents in the series, choose the [Format] Document command and type *0* in the Number Pages From: box. Word then sequentially numbers pages throughout the documents. If the first document ends on page 56, Word starts the second document on page 57, and so on, for all documents in the series.

Sequential footnotes

Open the first document in the series and note the number of the document's last footnote. Then open the next document in the series, choose the [Format] Document command, and type the next footnote number in the Footnotes Number From: box. Follow this procedure for each document in the series.

Sequential line numbers

If the lines in the document have been numbered, open the first document in the series and choose the [File] Print Preview command to see the document's last line number. Open the next document in the series, choose the [Format] Document command, and type the next line number in the Number Lines From: box. Follow this procedure for each document in the series.

Sequential paragraph numbers

Open the first document and select the paragraphs to be numbered. If you don't select anything, the entire document is numbered. Choose the [Utilities] Renumber command and note the last paragraph number. Open the next document and either select the paragraphs to be numbered or don't select any in order to number the entire document. Then choose the [Utilities] Renumber command, type the next paragraph number in the Start At: box, and click OK. Follow this procedure for each document in the series.

Printing linked documents

Open the first document in the series and choose the [File] Print command. In the Print dialog box, the Print Next File option is already checked. To start printing, click the OK button.

To print linked documents separately, click the Print Next File option to remove the check before clicking OK.

See also: Indexing, Table of contents

Linking styles

See: Next style

Mail

If your Macintosh is connected to a Microsoft Mail server on an AppleTalk network, you can send and receive formatted Word 4 files in the form of electronic mail messages without leaving Word. (Refer to your Microsoft Mail manual for details on using Microsoft Mail.) You can edit, format, and save files that you send and receive with the [File] Open Mail and Send Mail commands as you would regular Word 4 documents.

Sending Mail messages

Create your message as you would any Word 4 document and choose the [File] Send Mail command. Click the names of the people you want to receive the message, type a message title in the Re: box, and click Send. To be notified when people receive your message, check the Return Receipt box before you click Send. To keep a copy of the message, choose the [File] Save As command, type a name for the document/message, and click OK.

Reading Mail messages

Choose the [File] Open Mail command to display a list of the messages you've received and double-click the title of the message you want to read. (Titles for messages you haven't yet read appear in bold.) Word displays each message in its own document window. To display many messages at once, hold down the Shift key while you double-click the message titles. To save a message you've received, choose the [File] Save As command, type a name for the document/ message, and click OK.

Deleting Mail messages

Choose the [File] Open Mail command to display the list of messages, select the titles of the messages you want to delete (hold down the Shift key to select multiple messages), and click the Delete button.

Mailing labels

To print mailing labels, you create a data document and a main document and use the [File] Print Merge command. First, create a data document that contains a header record that names the fields (such as name, street, city, state, and zip) and the names and addresses you want to print on the labels. Separate the fields with commas and press the Return (or the Enter) key after each record except the last one. The following is an example data document called *Members*:

```
name, street, city, state, zip code
Andrew Fishbein, 8055 Elm St., Sunrise, FL, 33035
Bill Plaschke, 945 Jasmine Ct., Carlsbad, CA, 92009
Julie Bemaman, 555 North Ave, Fort Lee, NJ, 11358
Jim Daniel, 9597 Presidential, Utica, MI, 48572
```

Then follow the directions below for creating the main document appropriate for your printer and the label size.

ImageWriter, 1-column, 8.5" x 11" paper

Create a data document as described above. Then create a main document with 0.25-inch or 0.5-inch left margins that looks like this:

```
«DATA Members»«name»
«street»
«city», «state» «zip code»
```

To insert the special characters « and », choose the [Edit] Glossary command and double-click the entry *print merge* or press Option-\ (backslash) for « and Shift-Option-\ (backslash) for ».

ImageWriter, 3-columns, 8.5" x 11" paper

Create a data document as described above. Then create a main document with 0.25-inch or 0.5-inch left margins that looks like this:

```
«DATA Members»«name»
«street»
«city», «state» «zip code»
```

```
«name»
«street»
«city», «state» «zip code»
```

```
«name»
«street»
«city», «state» «zip code»
```

Then select the document and choose the [Format] Section command. Type *3* in the Columns Number: box, type *0* in the Spacing: box, select New Column under Start:, and click OK. You might also want to move the left indent marker on the ruler to about 0.25 inch to prevent addresses from printing at the far left edge of the labels.

Printing labels on ImageWriter

After creating the data document and the main document for one-column or three-column labels, choose the [Edit] Preferences command. Type *8.5* in the Custom Paper Size Width box and the height of a label (*1*, for example) in the Height box and click OK. If your labels are wider in total than 8.5 inches, type their exact total width in the Width box. Then choose the [File] Page Setup command under Paper: and select the Custom option. Check No Gaps Between Pages under Special Effects: and click the Document button. In the Document dialog box, set the top, bottom, and right margins to 0 and the left margin to 0.25 or 0.5 inch for both one-column and three-column labels. Click OK to exit the Document dialog box, and click OK again to exit the Page Setup dialog box.

To print the labels, load your label paper and line up the first label. Choose the [File] Print Merge command and click the Print button. If you print one column, each name and address in your data document will be printed once. If you print three columns, each name and address will be printed three times—once in each column.

LaserWriter, 1" or 1.5" labels

Create a data document as described earlier. Then create a main document that looks like this:

```
«DATA Members»¶
¶
«name»¶
«street»¶
«city», «state» «zip code»¶
¶
¶
¶
«NEXT»¶
«name»¶
«street»¶
«city», «state» «zip code»¶
¶
¶
```

```
«NEXT»¶
«name»¶
«street»¶
«city», «state» «zip code»¶
¶
¶
¶
«NEXT»¶
«name»¶
«street»¶
«city», «state» «zip code»¶
```

For 1-inch labels, repeat the «NEXT» groupings until you have 27
groupings. For 1.5-inch labels, repeat the «NEXT» groupings to a total
of 14. If you have fewer than 27 (or 14, for 1.5-inch labels) records in
your data document, Word will print only as many records as are
present.

The number of times you press the Return (or the Enter) key after
each «NEXT» grouping depends on the number of lines in your addresses and the height of your mailing labels:

Size of label	Number of lines in address	Press Return
1-inch	3 lines	3 times
1-inch	4 lines	2 times
1.5-inch	3 lines	6 times
1.5-inch	4 lines	5 times
1.5-inch	5 lines	4 times

Then select all the document's text and choose the [Format] Section
command. For 1-inch labels in three columns, type *3* in the Columns
Number: box and *0* in the Spacing: box and click OK. For 1.5-inch
labels in two columns, type *2* in the Columns Number: box and *0.5* in
the Spacing: box and click OK. To ensure that the LaserWriter prints
six lines per inch, choose the [Format] Paragraph command, type *–12
pt* in the Line: box, and click OK. Then choose the [Format] Document command and for 1-inch labels set the margins Top: and Bottom:
to 1 inch or 0.5 inch, and Left: and Right: to 0.5 inch. For 1.5-inch
labels, set margins Top: and Bottom: to 0.5 inch, Left: to 0.75 inch,
and Right: to 0.5 inch. You might have to experiment with the size of
the margins depending on how the labels are positioned on the page.

To print the labels, load your labels face down in the tray, choose the
[File] Print Merge command, and click the Print button.

Comments

If your 8.5-inch by 11-inch label sheets contain half-labels in the top and bottom rows, set the top and bottom margins to 0.5 inch and use only the full labels on the sheet. If your label sheets contain 11 rows of 1-inch labels, set the top and bottom margins to 1 inch. The printer will skip the first and last rows of labels. On a LaserWriter, these first and last rows are unusable because LaserWriters require a minimum margin of 0.5 inch.

See also: Print merge

Mail merge

See: Print merge

Margins

The margin is the space from the page edge to the beginning of text. In Word, you set top, bottom, left, and right margins for the entire document with the [Format] Document command, with the margin icon in Print Preview, or with the scale icon on the ruler. If you want to vary the amount of space surrounding individual paragraphs in a document, change the indents for those paragraphs by moving the indent markers on the ruler.

To set margins for your document, choose the [File] Print Preview command, click the margin icon, and drag the margin handles (the boxes at the end of the dotted lines) to where you want the margins. Note that the size of the margin appears at the top of the window as you drag the handles. Double-click to redraw the page with the new margins in Print Preview. Click Cancel or Page View to close Print Preview.

You can also set margins by choosing the [Format] Document command and typing the measurements you want or by clicking the scale icon on the ruler to change the ruler to page scale and dragging the square brackets to where you want the margins.

Margin bracket

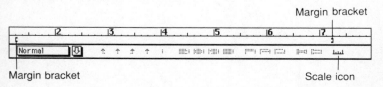

Margin bracket   Scale icon

Comments

The Apple LaserWriter requires minimum margins of 0.5 inch.

For binding facing pages

If you plan to put your document in a binder and make front-and-back copies, you'll need extra right and left margin space on even- and odd-numbered pages. Choose the [Format] Document command, choose from among the options described below, and click OK.

Mirror Even/Odd Margins Check this option to make even- and odd-numbered pages mirror images. The Left: and Right: options will change to Inside: and Outside:. The Inside: option determines the right margin of even-numbered pages and the left margin of odd-numbered pages. The Outside: option determines the left margin of even-numbered pages and the right margin of odd-numbered pages.

Gutter Type a measurement to add additional space at the inside margin only. If you type a gutter margin measurement and check Mirror Even/Odd Margins, Word adds the gutter space in addition to any measurement you might have typed for the inside margin. If you type a gutter margin but do not check Mirror Even/Odd Margins, the left and right margins of even-numbered and odd-numbered pages are the same and the gutter space is added to the right edge of even-numbered pages and the left edge of odd-numbered pages.

See also: Headers and footers, Ruler

Math   *Command-=*

To add, subtract, multiply, divide, or calculate percentages, type the appropriate operators between the numbers, select the numbers and operators, and choose the [Utilities] Calculate command. Word displays the result in the lower-left corner of the window and copies it to the Clipboard (so that you can paste it anywhere).

Use the following operators *before* numbers:

Addition	+ or no operator
Subtraction	− or parentheses around a number
Multiplication	*
Division	/

Use the calculate percentage operator (%) *after* the number.

If you select a column of numbers without operators (in a table, for example) and choose the [Utilities] Calculate command, Word adds the numbers. To select a column in a table, hold down the Option key and click inside the column. You can also select a column of numbers outside a table (numbers separated by tabs, for example) by holding down the Option key and dragging over the column.

If you surround a number with parentheses, that number becomes a negative number. If no operator precedes the parentheses in a list of numbers, the value is subtracted from the previous number.

Word calculates from left to right and from top to bottom. Do not use parentheses ( ) to group operations; put operations you want to be calculated first either at the top of a column or to the left. For example, Word calculates the expression

    10 + 10 + 5 * 2

as follows:

    10 + 10 = 20
    20 + 5 = 25
    25 * 2 = 50

The same numbers and operations in different order,

    5 * 2 + 10 + 10

produce a different answer:

    5 * 2 = 10
    10 + 10 = 20
    20 + 10 = 30

When calculating decimal places, Word displays the result with the same number of decimal places as the number in the equation with the most decimal places.

Measurements

In Word 4 you can specify these units of measurement for distances and positions of objects: inches (in or "), centimeters (cm), points (pt), or picas (pi). To change the default unit of measurement (inches) for all documents, choose the [Edit] Preferences command, select the unit of measurement you want from the Default Measure: box, and click OK. Word always displays the ruler and the position of objects in Page View or Print Preview in the current unit of measurement. You can type any unit of measurement for values in dialog boxes simply by typing its abbreviation after the number, regardless of the default unit of measurement set in Preferences.

Comments
For line, paragraph, text, and border spacing and for expanding, condensing, superscripting, or subscripting characters, the default unit of measurement is points (pt).

See also: Ruler

Merging documents

See: Print merge

Moving paragraphs

See: Positioning paragraphs

Moving text

To move text from one place to another in a document, select the text, choose the [Edit] Cut command, position the insertion point at the new location, and choose the [Edit] Paste command. When you choose the [Edit] Cut command, Word places a copy of the text on the Clipboard. To display the Clipboard's contents, choose the [Window] Show Clipboard command. If you want to copy the text without deleting it from its original location, choose the [Edit] Copy command instead of the [Edit] Cut command.

To bypass the Clipboard when you move text, select the text, press Option-Command-X, position the insertion point at the new location, and press the Return (or the Enter) key.

See also: Copying text, Deleting text, Editing, Inserting text, Tables

MultiFinder

With Apple Computer, Inc.'s MultiFinder you can run Microsoft Word
and another application at the same time and switch between them
without quitting one application in order to start the other. For information about installing, starting, and quitting MultiFinder, refer to
your MultiFinder manual.

To run MultiFinder, Word, and another application, you must have a
Macintosh with at least 1 MB of memory and an 800 KB external
drive or a hard disk. To run MultiFinder, Word, and Microsoft Excel
or other large applications, you must have 2 MB of memory. The
Word program alone has a recommended minimum of 512 KB of
memory.

To quickly transfer information from an application such as Microsoft
Excel to Microsoft Word, select the information in Microsoft Excel
that you want to copy and choose the [Edit] Copy command. Switch to
Word (either by clicking the icon in the upper-right corner of the
screen or by clicking inside the Word document window if it's visible). Position the insertion point in the Word document where you
want the information and choose the [Edit] Paste command. When you
are running MultiFinder, you can use Word's QuickSwitch feature to
easily update the transferred information.

See also: QuickSwitch

Multiplying

See: Math

Next style

You can define styles so that after you format the current paragraph
with one style and press the Return (or the Enter) key, another (next)
style is applied to the next paragraph.

To define a next style, choose the [Format] Define Styles command
and select the current style. In the Next Style: box, type the name for

the next style. Then click the Define button to define the next style and continue working in the dialog box or click OK to define the style and close the dialog box.

By assigning next styles, you can save keystrokes and automate the process of applying styles. For example, you might define a style called *displayhead* with the formats New York and 18 points. If every *displayhead* paragraph will be followed by text with the style *displaytext* with formats New York and 12 points, you can define *displaytext* as the next style. That way, after you type and apply the style *displayhead* to the first paragraph, the next paragraph will be formatted with the style *displaytext* when you press the Return (or the Enter) key.

The default next style is always the same as the current style because in most documents many paragraphs with the same style follow one another. For instance, in the example above, you'd probably want the next style for *displaytext* to be *displaytext* because you'd probably have more than one paragraph of text beneath each heading.

See also: Applying a style, Defining a style, Styles, Style sheets, Redefining a style

Numbering lines

To add line numbers to an entire document or to selected sections, select the entire document or only the sections in which you want line numbers. Then choose the [Format] Section command, choose from the following options under Line Numbers, and click OK:

By Page Restarts line numbers at 1 at the top of each new page.

By Section Restarts line numbers at 1 at the top of each new section.

Continuous Numbers lines sequentially throughout the entire document.

Count By: Lets you type a number by which to increment line numbers. Type *2*, for example, to number every second line or *10* to number every tenth line.

From Text: Type a measurement that specifies the distance you want between the line number and the beginning of the text. Auto leaves 0.25 inch between a line number and one text column or 0.13 inch between a line number and the text when there is more than one column of text.

Word adds line numbers to all lines in the document, including blank lines used for spacing. Word does not add line numbers to space specified with the Space Before: and Space After: options in the [Format] Paragraph dialog box. Word does not include tables, footnotes, headers, and footers in a line count.

To exclude line numbers from certain paragraphs in your document, select those paragraphs and choose the [Format] Paragraph command. Click Line Numbering to remove the check and click OK. Word inserts a paragraph properties mark (small black box) next to the paragraphs to indicate that they have special paragraph formatting. To see the paragraph properties mark, choose the [Edit] Show ¶ command.

You can see line numbers only in Print Preview and when you print the document. To see line numbers, choose the [File] Print Preview command and use the scroll bar at the right of the window to move through the document one page at a time.

See also: Counting

Numbering pages

See: Page numbers

Numbering paragraphs

To add numbers to the left of paragraphs, select the paragraphs you want to number or position the insertion point anywhere in the document to number all paragraphs in the document. Choose the [Utilities] Renumber command, select from the options described below, and click OK.

All Numbers all paragraphs in the selection, excluding empty paragraphs used for spacing. In Outline View, Word numbers only the expanded headings and text.

Only If Already Numbered Renumbers paragraphs that are already numbered.

Start At: Lets you type the starting number for the first paragraph to be numbered. If you are using non-Arabic formatted numbers or letters, type the corresponding Arabic number. For example, type *3* to start numbering at III (the sequence would continue with IV, V, VI,

and so on); type *6* to start numbering at F, the sixth letter of the
alphabet (the sequence would continue with G, H, I, J, and so on). For
multiple levels, type Arabic numbers for the level at which you want
to start numbering. For example, type *5.1* to start at 5.1 (the sequence
would continue with 5.2, 5.3, 5.4, and so on); type *6.1* and then type
A.1 in the Format: box (see below) to start at F.1 (the sequence would
continue with F.2, F.3, F.4, and so on).

Format: Type the following symbols to represent the formats of the
numbers you want to be displayed: *1* for arabic, *I* for uppercase Roman
numerals, *i* for lowercase Roman numerals, *A* for uppercase letters, or
a for lowercase letters. To include separators between numbers, you
can add commas, hyphens, slashes, semicolons, colons, parentheses,
braces, or brackets. If you don't add one of these separators, Word
places a period after the number. You can indicate different formats
for each level. For example, typing *I.A.1.a.* for the format results in
standard outline numbering.

Numbers: Click 1 to display only a single number for each paragraph
in a level. For example:

```
1              or     F
   1                     1
   2                     2
2                     G
```

Click 1.1 to display the previous superior numbers in the sequence with
the number of the paragraph in the level. For example:

```
1              or     F.1
2                     F.1.1
   2.1                F.1.2
   2.2              F.2
3                  F.3
```

Click By Example to use either the 1 or the 1.1 scheme based on the
number in the first paragraph of the selection.

When you number indented paragraphs, the default format is Arabic
numerals for each level. If you don't indicate a format for a particular
level, Word bases the default number format on how far to the right a
paragraph is indented.

When you use the Renumber command in Outline View, Word numbers only expanded (displayed) paragraphs.

To remove numbers from paragraphs, select the paragraphs, choose
the [Utilities] Renumber command, click Remove, and click OK.

Examples

Below are some common numbering schemes and the Renumber dialog box settings used to achieve them.

Settings:
Type *1* in the Start At: box, type *1)* in the Format: box, and click 1 under Numbers.

Result:

   1)
   2)
   3)

Settings:
Type *1* in the Start At: box, type *1.1.1* in the Format: box, and click 1.1 under Numbers.

Result:

   1.1
   1.2
      1.2.1
      1.2.2
   1.3

Settings:
Type *1* in the Start At: box, type *I.A.* in the Format box, and click 1.1 under Numbers.
Result:

   I.
   II.
      II.A.
      II.B.
   III.

Opening a document   *Command-O*

To open a new document, choose the [File] New command.

To open an existing document, choose the [File] Open command and double-click the name of the document you want to open. If you want to open the document as a read-only file (you will be unable to make changes to the file), click the Read Only box before you double-click the name of the document. The amount of available disk space determines the number of documents you can have open at one time. The maximum number of documents you can have open is 22.

The Open dialog box displays Macintosh folders, Word files, files with the Macintosh TEXT format, Microsoft Works, MacWrite, and MacPaint files, and files with the Microsoft Interchange Format (RTF). When you open an RTF file, Word asks if you want to open the file as a text file (no formatting) or as a Word 4 file with Word formatting.

To display all the files on the current disk, hold down the Shift key while you choose the [File] Open Any File command. If you double-click a file with a format other than one of the types listed above, Word interprets the file as text only (ASCII).

See also: QuickSwitch, Windows

Outlining $Command\text{-}U$

Outlining is a view of the structure of your document in which headings are indented according to their places in the document's hierarchy. It's a good idea to create an outline for a document that has many heading levels such as a report or a book. Because the changes you make in Outline View are maintained when you switch to another view, you can quickly reorganize your document by moving only the headings in Outline View. To switch to Outline View, choose the [Document] Outlining command. To switch back to Galley View, choose the [Document] Outlining command again.

Creating an outline

To create an outline, choose the [Document] Outlining command, type the first heading, and press the Return (or the Enter) key. Before you type each heading, click the left or right arrow icon to indent the heading and assign a heading level. To type body text below the heading, click the body text icon before you type.

Collapsing and expanding subheadings

In Outline View, headings that have subheadings are marked with a plus sign icon, headings without subheadings have a minus sign icon, and body text has a small square icon. To collapse (hide) or expand (display) a subheading, double-click the plus sign icon next to the heading. A heading with collapsed subheadings has a wavy, dotted underline. To collapse or expand to a specific level of heading (for example, to display all the level 3 headings), click the 1, 2, 3, or 4 icon at the top of the screen. You can also click the show all levels icon to show all levels of your outline, the ellipsis icon to display only the first line of the body text followed by an ellipsis (...), or the formatting icon to display the outline without its formatting.

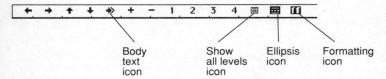

Body text icon   Show all levels icon   Ellipsis icon   Formatting icon

Moving, promoting, and demoting headings

To move a heading and its subheadings, drag the heading's plus sign icon up or down to the new position. Subheadings are attached to their headings and move along with the headings regardless of whether they have been expanded (displayed). Move body text or headings without subheadings in the same way. To move a heading without moving its attached subheadings, hold down the Option key and then drag the heading's plus sign icon.

You can also use the Cut and Paste commands to move headings and body text. Select the headings or body text and choose the [Edit] Cut command. Scroll to the new location, position the insertion point, and choose the [Edit] Paste command.

To change a heading to body text, select the heading and click the body text icon.

To promote a heading to a higher level, drag its icon to the left. To demote a heading to a lower level, drag its icon to the right. When you promote or demote headings, you change their assigned styles as well as move them to the left or right.

Automatic styles in an outline

Each outline heading is assigned an automatic style (*heading 1* through *heading 9*). Body text is initially assigned *Normal* style. If you are working with a long document with many heading levels, it's a good idea to use the *heading 1* through *heading 9* styles for your headings in Galley View so that they are linked to your outline. (Text with any other style is treated as body text when you switch to Outline View.) Formats for heading styles are preassigned, but you can change them. To change a preassigned heading style, choose the [Document]

Outlining command to return to Galley View and format one of the headings you want to change. Then choose the [Format] Show Ruler command, choose that heading level from the style box, click the Redefine the style based on selection option, and click OK. You can also use the [Format] Define Styles command to redefine the automatic outline styles.

Because of the link between outline headings and styles, when you promote or demote a heading in Outline View, it receives the automatic style for that heading; likewise, when you apply a different automatic heading style in Galley View, the heading is promoted or demoted accordingly when you return to Outline View.

Numbering outline headings

Select the outline, choose the [Utilities] Renumber command, type *1* in the Start At: box, type *I.A.1.a.* (no spaces) in the Format box, and click OK. Word does not number body text even though you have selected it.

Printing an outline

Choose the [Document] Outlining command to switch to Outline View. Expand or collapse the headings until everything you want to print is shown, and choose the [File] Print command.

See also: Automatic styles, Numbering paragraphs, Styles, Table of contents

Outlining styles

See: Automatic styles

Page breaks   *Shift-Enter*

You can insert automatic or manual page breaks or have Word paginate in the background as you type. You can also change page breaks in Print Preview. To paginate your document, first choose the [Document] Repaginate Now command, then scroll to see if all the page breaks are where you want them. To change a page break, click at the start of a paragraph above the automatic break that Word inserted and press Shift-Enter or choose the [Document] Insert Page Break command to add a manual page break. Then choose the [Document] Repaginate Now command again to repaginate from that point to the end of the document. Continue scrolling to check page breaks and add manual page breaks (Shift-Enter) as needed.

Automatic page breaks

To have Word paginate a document after you've typed it, choose the [Document] Repaginate Now command. Word also repaginates whenever you choose the [Document] Page View or [File] Print Preview command. Word's automatic page breaks look like this in Galley View:

Word inserts automatic page breaks depending on page size, margins, font size, line spacing, and other formats in your document. Whenever you edit your document, automatic page breaks are adjusted accordingly. You cannot delete an automatic page break in Galley View. To change the automatic page break, insert a manual page break above or below the automatic break by pressing Shift-Enter. Then repaginate by choosing the [Document] Repaginate Now command.

To control placement of automatic page breaks in a paragraph, select the paragraph and choose the [Format] Paragraph command. Then choose from the options described below, and click OK.

Keep With Next Prevents a page break from separating the paragraph from the following paragraph.

Page Break Before Ensures that the paragraph always starts a new page (handy for major headings).

Keep Lines Together Keeps all the lines in the paragraph on the same page (handy for tables and paragraphs with borders).

To prevent a single line from being separated from the rest of a paragraph by a page break (which makes it a *widow*), choose the [Format] Document command, check Widow Control, and click OK.

Manual page breaks

To insert a manual page break, press Shift-Enter. A manual page break looks like this in Galley View:

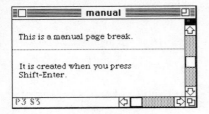

Word doesn't adjust manual page breaks when you make formatting changes to your document that affect pagination. To delete a manual page break, select it and press Backspace.

Background repagination

To have Word update page breaks whenever you stop typing or editing, choose the [Edit] Preferences command, click Background Repagination, and click OK. Note that certain editing and formatting tasks will be slower when Background Repagination is turned on.

Changing page breaks in Print Preview

In Print Preview, automatic page breaks are shown as thin dotted lines after you click the margins icon; manual page breaks are shown as darker gray dotted lines. To move an automatic page break in Print Preview, choose the [File] Print Preview command, click the margins icon, and drag the page break up or down. When you drag an automatic page break up or down, Word inserts a manual break at the new location.

Comments

When you change printers, you might need to force automatic pagination for a document in order to account for the new printer settings. (When you choose the [Document] Repaginate Now command, Word determines whether or not pagination is needed based only on changes made to the document, and it might not repaginate.) To force Word to repaginate, hold down the Shift key while choosing the [Document] Full Repaginate Now command.

If you alternate between printers, use Chooser to select the current printer before paginating your document because the print width of characters can vary from printer to printer, thus affecting page breaks.

Page layout

See: Formatting, Formatting sections, Page View

Page numbers

You can add page numbers to a document in Print Preview, as part of a header or footer, or with the [Format] Section command.

In Print Preview

To position page numbers at the default position (0.5 inch from the top and right page edges), choose the [File] Print Preview command and double-click the page number icon. To position page numbers in a different position, click the page number icon, drag the number pointer to the location, and click. To remove page numbers, click the margins icon, drag the page number off the page, and click outside the page to redraw the page.

To change the page number format, click the Print Preview Cancel button to return to Galley View or Page View. Choose the [Format] Define Styles command and select the style *page number* from the list box. Choose commands from the Character, Format, and Font menus to change the formats for the style, and click OK.

To add text to the page number (such as A-1 or ****1****), create the page number in a header or footer. (See below.)

As part of a header or footer

To add page numbers as part of a header or footer or to add text to the page number (such as A-1 or ****1****), choose the [Document] Open Header or Open Footer command. Type the text for the header or footer, and position the insertion point where you want the page number to be. Note that it might be necessary to add tabs or spaces in order to position the insertion point where you want the page number. Type any page number text that will precede the number, click the page number icon, and then type any page number text that you want to follow the number. To close the header or footer window, click the close box. To remove page numbers, choose the [Document] Open Header or Open Footer command, select the page number and any accompanying text, and press Backspace.

To change the page number format, select the page number in the header or footer window and choose commands from the Character, Format, and Font menus.

Comments

Do not add a page number to the header or footer if you've already added a page number in Print Preview; if you do, the document will contain two sets of page numbers.

With the [Format] Section command

Use the [Format] Section command when you want different page numbering schemes for different sections of a document. Position the insertion point in the section you want to number and choose the [Format] Section command. Select from the following options under Page Number and click OK. You can also use the following options to reposition page numbers already added with Print Preview or as part of a header or footer.

Auto Adds page numbers. Do not check Auto if you've already added page numbers in the header or footer; if you do, two sets of page numbers will be displayed.

Restart at 1 Restarts page numbers at 1 in this section, or at I, i, A, or a, depending on the format.

1 2 3 Numbers pages with Arabic numerals.

I II III Numbers pages with uppercase Roman numerals.

i ii iii Numbers pages with lowercase Roman numerals.

A B C Numbers pages with uppercase letters.

a b c Numbers pages with lowercase letters.

From Top: Specifies the distance from the top of the page to the top of an automatic page number. Type in the distance you want.

From Right: Specifies the distance from the right edge of the page to the left edge of the page number. Type in the distance you want. If you selected Mirror Even/Odd Margins in the Document dialog box, left-page numbers are positioned from the left edge of the page to the right edge of the page number.

To change the page number format, choose the [Format] Define Styles command and select the style *page number* from the list box. Choose commands from the Character, Format, and Font menus to change the formats for the style, and click OK.

See also: Headers and footers, Linking documents, Title page

Page View

Command-B

Choose the [Document] Page View command to see a full-size view of how your document will look when it is printed. In Page View, elements appear in their actual positions on the page—headers and footers, footnotes, page numbers, multiple columns, and positioned text and graphics. You can type, edit, and choose commands in Page View just as you can in Galley View. As you type and edit in Page View, Word wraps lines of text and, if necessary, moves text to the next page. Typing and editing is faster in Galley View, so it's a good idea to create documents in Galley View and then refine and lay out pages in Page View.

To scroll to other pages in Page View, click the page forward icon to move forward one page and click the page back icon to move back one page.

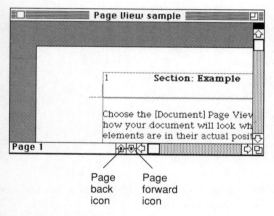

Page
back
icon

Page
forward
icon

To have documents open in Page View instead of Galley View when you choose the [File] Open command, choose the [Edit] Preferences command, check Open Documents in Page View, and click OK. To display text boundaries in Page View so that you can see the layout of a page more clearly, choose the [Edit] Preferences command, check Show Text Boundaries in Page View, and click OK. Page View text boundaries are also displayed when you choose the [Edit] Show ¶ command.

To return to Galley View, choose the [Document] Page View command again.

Comments

In Page View, Word repaginates only up to the current page unless you specify Background Repagination in the [Edit] Preferences dialog box. If you don't specify Background Repagination, update the current page by choosing the [Document] Repaginate Now command.

See also: Editing, Galley View, Print Preview

Paragraph formatting

See: Formatting paragraphs

Paragraph mark   *Return or Enter*

A paragraph mark (¶) designates the end of a paragraph. To display paragraph marks and other special symbols (for spaces, tabs, cell marks, and so on), choose the [Edit] Show ¶ command. Word inserts a paragraph mark every time you press the Return (or the Enter) key.

Each paragraph mark stores formats or styles or both for that paragraph; consequently, even if you delete all the text in a paragraph, any new text you type receives the deleted paragraph's formats if you did not delete the paragraph mark. To delete a paragraph mark, select it and press Backspace.

See also: Formatting paragraphs, Line breaks

Pasting

See: Moving text

Picas

See: Measurements

Points

See: Measurements

Positioning paragraphs

With the [Format] Position command you can position text, graphics, a table, or rows in a table a specified distance from the page edge or the margin or both. You can position a graphic in the center of the page, for example, and have text flow around it; or you can position comments about the main text in the margin. When you position a paragraph with the [Format] Position command, Word places the paragraph outside the typical sequential flow of paragraphs.

To position a paragraph, select the paragraph, choose the [Format] Position command, choose from among the options described below, and click OK.

Horizontal Specifies the horizontal alignment of the paragraph. Type a measurement to indicate the horizontal alignment of the paragraph (from the page edge, left margin, or text column) or select from the following list. Choosing Left aligns the left edge of the paragraph with the page edge, left margin, or text column. If you choose Left and click the Relative to: Page option, Word places the paragraph in the left margin. Choosing Center centers the paragraph between the left and right margins. Choosing Right aligns the right edge of the paragraph with the page edge, right margin, or text column. If you choose Right and click the Relative to: Page option, Word places the paragraph in the right margin. Choosing Inside is the same as choosing Left for odd-numbered pages and Right for even-numbered pages. Choosing Outside is the same as choosing Right for odd-numbered pages and Left for even-numbered pages.

Horizontal Relative to: Specifies the element from which horizontal paragraph positioning will be measured. Choose Margin to position the paragraph horizontally between the left and right margins and within the main text area. Choose Page to position the paragraph horizontally in the margin (Left, Right, Inside, Outside, or with a measurement you type). Choose Center Relative to Margin to center the paragraph between the left and right margins of the page.

Vertical Specifies the vertical alignment of the paragraph. Type a measurement to indicate the vertical alignment of the paragraph (from the top of the page or from the top margin) or select from the following list. Choosing Inline places the paragraph on the page sequentially, following the normal order of paragraphs. Choosing Top aligns the top edge of the paragraph with the top margin or top edge of the page. Choosing Center centers the paragraph between margins or edges of the page. Choosing Bottom aligns the bottom of the paragraph with the bottom margin or the bottom edge of the page.

Vertical Relative to: Specifies the element from which vertical paragraph positioning will be measured. Choose Margin to position the paragraph vertically between the top and bottom margins and within the main text area. Choose Page to position the paragraph between the top and bottom edges of the page. These options have no effect if Inline is chosen for Vertical.

Distance From Text: Specifies a positioned paragraph's relationship to surrounding text. Type a measurement for the distance between the boundaries of the positioned paragraph and the text of normal surrounding paragraphs.

Paragraph Width: Specifies the width of the positioned paragraph. The default is Auto, which makes the paragraph's width the same as the width of the main text column. If you want a different width for the positioned paragraph, type the width in the Paragraph Width: box. If you want to contain a paragraph in the left or right margin, make the paragraph's width the same as the margin's width.

To reset the settings in the [Format] Position dialog box so that the paragraph is no longer positioned, click the Reset button. You can also select the paragraph and press Command-Shift-P to remove any positioning.

To position a paragraph as you view the layout of the page, choose the [Format] Position command, select from among the options above (approximating the position you want), and click the Preview button. Click the margins icon and drag the paragraph to the exact location on the page. When you have positioned the paragraph, click either Cancel or Page View to retain the positioning and return to editing your document.

After you position a paragraph, Word places a paragraph properties mark (a small black box) to its left indicating that it is a positioned paragraph. To display the mark, choose the [Edit] Show ¶ command. To quickly display the [Format] Position dialog box, double-click the paragraph properties mark.

PostScript

PostScript, developed by Adobe Systems Incorporated, is a page description language for Apple LaserWriters and laserprinters and typesetters compatible with PostScript. To learn how to use PostScript, refer to the *PostScript Language Tutorial and Cookbook* and the *PostScript Language Reference Manual* by Adobe Systems Incorporated (Addison-Wesley). The following paragraphs describe elements of PostScript specific to Word.

If you have a PostScript printer, you can include PostScript commands in Word documents to create special text or graphics such as company logos or gray-shaded borders. To use PostScript in Word documents, you must apply the automatic style *PostScript* to the commands: Select a PostScript command or group of commands and either choose the [Format] Define Styles command or press the Shift key and choose the [Format] Define All Styles command. *PostScript* is an automatic style, which means that it is not included in the Define Styles list box until you type its name in the Style box. *PostScript* does appear in the Define All Styles list box. Type *PostScript* in the style box or choose PostScript from the list box, and click OK. Word adds the style *PostScript* to the style box on the ruler and to the list box (if it's not already there). To continue applying the style *PostScript*, select the other PostScript commands and choose PostScript from the style box on the ruler.

The style *PostScript* has the formats Normal, 10 point, Bold, and Hidden Text. You can change any format in the style definition except Hidden Text. If PostScript commands are not formatted as Hidden Text, Word will print the instructions instead of carrying them out.

To display the hidden PostScript commands, choose the [Edit] Preferences command, check Show Hidden Text, and click OK.

To print a document that contains PostScript commands, choose the [File] Print command, click Print Hidden Text to delete its check, and click OK. Because PostScript commands are interpreted and drawn before Word text and graphics, any Word text or graphics in the same position as a PostScript graphic will overlap or cover it. To print PostScript text or graphics on top of Word text or graphics (for example, to position PostScript arrows within an imported graphic), choose the [File] Page Setup command, check Print PostScript Over Text, and follow the directions above for printing.

If you are using a print spooler or MultiFinder's Background Printing option, the PostScript graphics on the first page will be shifted down and to the right. To correct this, turn off the print spooler or Background Printing and reprint only the first page.

The drawing rectangle and the coordinate system

In a Word document, you specify one of four commands that control the rectangle in which PostScript commands will draw (the drawing rectangle): within a page (.page.), within a paragraph (.para.), within a cell (.cell.) or within a graphics frame (.pic.). PostScript commands start drawing at the lower-left corner (graphics origin 0,0) of one of these areas. Positive numbers denote directions to the right and upward. When used before a table row, the .para. command applies to the entire row.

To change the position of the graphics origin of the drawing rectangle, use the PostScript command *translate*. To give the drawing rectangle a new shape, use the *clip* command to specify the new drawing area. Note that the new area must be contained in the old one. Use the *initclip* command to extend the current drawing area to the entire page. When you use the *initclip* command, the graphic origin remains at the lower-left corner of the drawing rectangle you originally specified.

Using page dictionaries

Use the .dict. operator in a header to create a PostScript group that contains definitions and procedures for all pages in your document. If you are using a LaserWriter driver earlier than version 5.0, you might not be able to use .dict. groups.

Special Word variables

You can use the following predefined Word variables along with PostScript commands. All distance measurements are in points.

For .page., .para., .cell., or .pic.

wp$page	(current page number)
wp$date	(current date)
wp$time	(current time)
wp$box	(path of the current drawing rectangle)
wp$x	(width of the drawing rectangle)
wp$y	(height of the drawing rectangle)
wp$xorig	(left edge of the drawing rectangle)
wp$yorig	(bottom edge of the drawing rectangle)

For .page. only

wp$top	(top margin)
wp$bottom	(bottom margin)
wp$left	(left margin, including gutter)
wp$right	(right margin, including gutter)
wp$col	(number of columns)
wp$colx	(width of each column)
wp$colxb	(space between columns)

For .para. or .cell. only

wp$top	(space before the paragraph or the first paragraph in the cell)
wp$bottom	(space after the paragraph or the first paragraph in the cell)
wp$left	(distance between the left margin and the left indent)
wp$right	(distance between the right margin and the right indent)
wp$style	(style name)
wp$first	(first indent)

Avoiding reset operators

Do not use PostScript operators that reset your printer or the Post-Script environment because they can interfere with regular Word text and graphics on the page. Avoid the following operators: banddevice, copypage, framedevice, grestoreall, initgraphics, initmatrix, nulldevice, renderbands, and showpage.

Importing Adobe Illustrator graphics

To import the PostScript commands from an Adobe Illustrator document into a Word document, hold down the Shift key and choose the [File] Open Any File command in Word to see the Illustrator files. Double-click the Illustrator file, select the PostScript commands you want, choose the [Edit] Copy command, and open your Word document. Position the insertion point at the location for the PostScript graphic and choose the [Edit] Paste command. Then determine the origin for the drawing rectangle by finding the PostScript comments with the form *%%Bounding Box:* x y # #, where *x*, *y*, and # are numbers. Type at the beginning of the imported PostScript commands the command -x -y *translate*, where $-x$ and $-y$ are the negative values of the x and y in the Bounding Box comment. This translates the graphics origin to (0,0). Then apply the style *PostScript* to all the PostScript commands.

To copy the PostScript images into a Word document, start Adobe Illustrator, select the graphic you want to copy, press the Option key, and choose the [Edit] Copy command. Switch to Word, open the document in which you want to insert the graphic, position the insertion point, and choose the [Edit] Paste command. In Word, the graphic is displayed as a bit map. The PostScript version of the graphic prints when you print the Word document.

Preferences

Options in the [Edit] Preferences dialog box control default settings for documents. When you change these settings, Word remembers the altered default settings and uses them the next time you start Word. To change the default settings, choose the [Edit] Preferences command, choose from among the following options, and click the OK button:

Default Measure: Choose a unit of measurement that will be the default for the measurements you type into option boxes in dialog boxes. The ruler is also displayed in the default unit of measurement—inches, centimeters, points, or picas.

Show Hidden Text Check this option to display hidden text in your document with a dotted underline. To hide such text, click the option to remove the check.

Use Picture Placeholders Check this option to display gray boxes in place of graphics on the screen in order to speed up scrolling. To display graphics on the screen, click the option to remove the check. When you print, the graphic prints regardless of whether this box is checked.

Show Table Gridlines Check this option to display dotted boundaries around tables. To remove the gridlines, click the option to remove the check. (Gridlines are also displayed if you have chosen the [Edit] Show ¶ command.)

Open Documents in Page View Check this option to display documents in Page View when you open them. To display documents in Galley View, click the option to remove the check.

Background Repagination Check this option to have Word repaginate every time you stop typing, editing, or formatting the document.

"Smart" Quotes Check this option to substitute typeset quality quotation marks every time you type " or '.

Keep Program in Memory: Check this option to speed up operation of the Word program by keeping Word in memory. Check Now to load as much of the Word program as possible into available memory for the current work session. Check Always to load as much of the program as possible into memory for all work sessions.

Keep File in Memory: Check this option to speed up operation of the Word program by keeping documents in memory. Check Now to load as much of the opened documents as possible into memory for the current work session. Check Always to load as much of the opened documents as possible into memory for all work sessions.

Custom Paper Size: Type a width and a height for odd-sized paper you want to use with Apple ImageWriter printers.

See also: Graphics, Hidden text, Measurements, Page breaks, Page View, Quotation marks, Tables

Printers

Microsoft Word works with any printer you can connect to your Macintosh, including ImageWriter, ImageWriter II, LaserWriter, LaserWriter Plus, LaserWriter II, several serial printers, and printers connected to a network. When you install Word, you should copy the appropriate printer driver into your System folder. A printer driver is special Macintosh system software that provides Word with information about a particular printer.

The following paragraphs describe how to set up various printers to work with Word.

ImageWriter printers

Make sure your printer is connected, choose the [Apple] Chooser command, and click the ImageWriter icon. Click the icon for the port (printer or modem) your printer is attached to, and click the close box.

Note: Do not select the modem port if you have a hard disk attached to the modem port—the hard disk might get erased.

LaserWriter printers

After you're sure that your printer is connected, you need to install the printing resources (similar to a printer driver), install the LaserWriter screen fonts (if necessary), and select LaserWriter with Chooser.

First, if you haven't installed the printing resources from the Finder, open the Installer program that came with your LaserWriter. Select your startup disk (with the System and Finder), select LaserWriter from the list box, and click the Install button. Next, check to see if the fonts you want to use have been installed: Choose the [Format] Character command and click the Font box to see the list of fonts and the Size box to see the list of font sizes. To install more fonts and sizes, open the Font/DA Mover utility, choose the Font option, and open the LaserWriter font file or another System file that contains the fonts you want. Select the fonts you want to copy and click the Copy button. To select LaserWriter as the printer, choose the [Apple] Chooser command, click the LaserWriter icon, and close the dialog box.

Serial printers

You can use serial printers such as AppleDaisy, Brother, Diablo 630, NEC 7710, and TTY with Word. To obtain the printer drivers for these printers, send the serial printer resource card included in your Word 4 package to Microsoft Corporation.

AppleTalk network printers

Install the AppleTalk ImageWriter or AppleTalk LaserWriter printing resources by following the instructions above for LaserWriter printers. Then choose the [Apple] Chooser command and click the icon for the AppleTalk ImageWriter or the AppleTalk LaserWriter. If you are networked to multiple zones, select the zone that lists the printer you want to use, select the name of the printer you want to use, and click the close box.

See also: Installing Word, Printing a document

Printing a document   *Command-P*

To print a document, first select the printer that is connected to your Macintosh: Choose the [Apple] Chooser command, click the printer's icon, and select the name of the printer you want to use. Then choose

the [File] Page Setup command, choose from among the available options, and click OK. (Each time you print, Word uses these settings as
the default.) Choose the [File] Print command, choose from among the
available options, and click OK. The options available in the Page
Setup dialog box and the Print dialog box vary depending on which
printer you are using. The following sections describe the options
common to most printers (standard options) and then specific options
for ImageWriter and LaserWriter printers. Check your printer manual
for details about options not listed here.

Standard page setup options

Paper Specifies the type of paper you'll print on. Choose US Letter for
8½" x 11", US Legal for 8½" x 14", A4 Letter for 8¼" x 11⅔", or Custom. If you have chosen the [Edit] Preferences command and typed
the paper's width and height in the Custom Size Paper boxes, the Custom option will be present in the Page Setup dialog box.

Orientation Specifies the paper's orientation. Click the vertical orientation icon to print across the width of the page (portrait orientation).
To print across the length of the page (landscape orientation), click the
horizontal orientation icon.

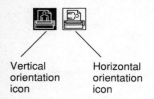

Vertical   Horizontal
orientation   orientation
icon   icon

Document Displays the [Format] Document dialog box, in which you
can specify margins and other document settings if necessary.

ImageWriter page setup options

Special Effects: Specifies proportions and other special printing re-
quirements. Choose Tall Adjusted to print graphics in correct propor-
tion, 50% Reduction to reduce the image on the page by 50%, or No
Gaps Between Pages to print over the perforation between pages.

LaserWriter page setup options

Reduce or Enlarge: Specifies the percentage from 25% through 400%
by which to reduce or enlarge text and graphics on the page. Type in
the percentage you want.

Font Substitution Substitutes LaserWriter fonts wherever non-LaserWriter fonts are used. (For example, substitute Times for New York.)

Text Smoothing Ensures that the edges of bit-mapped fonts are improved.

Graphics Smoothing Ensures that the edges of bit-mapped graphics are improved.

Faster Bitmap Printing Speeds up printing of bit-mapped graphics in a document.

Fractional Widths Improves the spacing of text in LaserWriter fonts. Printing is improved on paper, but the text on the screen might be distorted.

Print PostScript Over Text Prints Word text and graphics first, and then PostScript graphics on top.

Options Opens the dialog box that contains the extended LaserWriter options. Check Flip Horizontal or Flip Vertical to reverse the image or to print a graphic upside down. Check Invert Image to turn white to black and black to white. Check Precision Bitmap Alignment to reduce text and graphics to 96% to account for the 4–1 difference in pixel density between the LaserWriter (300 dots per inch) and the Macintosh (72 dots per inch). When you aren't downloading fonts, check Larger Print Area to make better use of memory and enable the LaserWriter to store larger images. When you are downloading many fonts, check Unlimited Downloadable Fonts in a Document.

Standard print options

Page Range: Click All to print all the pages in a document, or type a range of page numbers. To print from a particular page to the end of the document, specify in the From: box the page at which you want to begin the printing and leave the To: box empty. To print one page, type the same number in both boxes.

Copies: Type the number of copies you want to print.

Paper Source (Feed): Choose Automatic (ImageWriter) or Paper Cassette (LaserWriter) if the printer feeds paper. Choose Hand Feed (ImageWriter) or Manual Feed (LaserWriter) if you are inserting paper by hand. Word will pause and wait for you to insert each page. To continue printing after you have inserted a page, click the Continue button.

Section Range: Type a range of numbers for the sections you want to print. For example, to print only the pages in sections 2 and 3, type *2* and *3*.

Print Selection Only Check this option to print only the text currently selected.

Print Hidden Text Check this option to print text with the hidden text format. Click this option again to remove the check and ensure that PostScript commands are carried out and not printed.

Print Next File Check this option to print a series of linked documents as if they were one. Specify the next file by using the [Format] Document command.

ImageWriter print options

Quality: Choose Best to print high quality, slow speed; Faster to print standard quality, standard speed; or Draft to print without character or paragraph formatting but at fastest speed.

LaserWriter print options

Cover Page: Choose No to print without a cover page, First Page to print a cover page as the first page of a document, or Last Page to print a cover page as the last page of a document. A cover page gives information such as the date, document title, and user name.

Print Back to Front Check this option to print the document from the last page to the first page so that pages are in the correct order in the paper tray. Printing is slower when this option is checked.

Comments

If you alternate between printers, use Chooser to select the current printer before laying out or paginating your document. Line breaks and page breaks might change when you change printers because the print width of characters can vary from printer to printer. (For example, the print width of characters on the ImageWriter is narrower than the print width of characters on the LaserWriter.)

Print merge

Print merge is the process of printing a series of documents that have some text in common and some text that varies. For example, you might want to print form letters informing your clients of a rate increase. You type the body of the letter once in a main document and the names and addresses of your clients in a data document. The data document includes a header record that contains field names for each element. For example, *name* might be the field name for each client's name. The main document includes with each field name placeholders that indicate where Word will merge the information (for example, Dear «name»). When you are ready to print, choose the [File] Print Merge command and Word merges the names and addresses with the main document and prints one letter for each client.

To create the main document

Type the common text, or main document, leaving placeholders at the points where Word will bring in the text from the data document (for example, the name and address of each client). To insert a placeholder, press Option-\ (backslash) to insert the special character «, type the field name, and press Shift-Option-\ (backslash) to insert the special character ». A field name can contain up to 254 characters between the « and » symbols. The first paragraph in the main document must be a placeholder with the DATA instruction that tells Word the filename of the data document.

Example main document

«DATA Clients»

June 25, 1989

«addressee»
«address»
«city», «state» «zip code»

Dear «addressee»,

Beginning August 1, 1989, the cost for basic cable service will be increased to $15.95 per month.

Sincerely,

Howard Berber
Berber Cablevision.

In the main document, you can include any of the following merge instructions. Italics indicate a variable you replace with information. Note that a *field* variable cannot have the same name as a field in the header record of your data document.

«DATA *data document*»
«DATA *header document, data document*»

tells Word the name of the data document and the name of the header document (if included) that contains the header record. Create a separate header document if you want to use the same header record with different data documents or if you use your data document for purposes other than merging and you don't want to include a first-line header record in it. For example, you might have several client address documents and not want to bother typing a header record at the start of each one.

«ASK *field=?*»
«ASK *field=?message*»

prompts you for information to add to your document before printing. For example, you can have Word prompt you with your own message by including the following:

«ASK name=?Type name for salutation»

«SET *field=data*»
«SET *field=?*»
«SET *field=?message*»

sets a field equal to the data you type as you compose the instruction or prompts you for information to add to your document before printing. For example, you might type one general product introductory offer letter and then vary the type of product for each mailing:

«SET product=Home Cinema»

The last two SET commands work in the same way as the ASK commands.

«IF *field=data*»*result*«ENDIF»
«IF *field=data*»*result*«ELSE»*alternate result*«ENDIF»

IF, ENDIF prints the result if the condition you specify is met. If the condition is not met, no result is printed. IF, ELSE, ENDIF prints the result if the condition you specify is met. If the condition is not met, Word prints the alternative result. For either instruction, you can use these operators in place of the equal sign: >, >=, <, <=, or <>. For example:

```
«IF number > 2»You will continue to receive a 10%
discount for subscribing to more than two movie
channels.«ELSE»It's not too late to subscribe to two
movie channels to receive our 10% discount on total
services. Call 444-5666 today! «ENDIF»
```

«INCLUDE *document name*»

inserts in the main document all text from the document specified by *document name*. A document that is included in another with an INCLUDE instruction can contain an INCLUDE instruction itself, making it possible to chain up to 55 documents. You can also use INCLUDE in documents other than print merge documents.

«NEXT»

skips to the next data record. When you combine it with the IF instruction, you can use NEXT to specify a conditional range for printing. For example:

```
«IF status = cancel order»«NEXT»«ENDIF»
```

To create the data document

As the first line of the document, type a header record. The header record contains the field names (separated by commas or tabs) that you used as placeholders in the main document. Then type the data, separated by commas or tabs, pressing the Return (or the Enter) key only after you've typed each entire data record.

Example data document (Clients)

```
addressee, address, city, state, zip code
Andrew Fishbein, 8055 Elm St., Sunrise, FL, 33035
Bill Plaschke, 945 Jasmine Ct., Carlsbad, CA, 92009
Julie Bemaman, 555 North Ave., Fort Lee, NJ, 11358
Jim Daniel, 9597 Presidential, Utica, MI, 48572
```

Header records and data records can include as many as 127 field names and fields. The number of fields in the data record must be equal to the number of field names in the header record. To include quotation marks as part of a field, type in an extra set of quotation marks.

You must include the name of the data document in the DATA statement in the first paragraph of the main document. Do not use commas in the name of the data document.

To print the merged documents

Be sure the data document and the main document are on the same disk or in the same folder. Open the main document, choose the [File] Print Merge command, and choose from among the following options:

All Prints one document for each data record in the data document.

From: To: Prints one document for each data record included in the range you specify.

Print Displays the Print dialog box. Choose from among the print options and click the OK button to print the merged documents.

New Document Creates a new document called Form Letters that contains all the merged documents. You can preview, edit, or save this document.

See also: Mailing labels, Printing a document

Print Preview   *Command-I*

To see entire pages of a document as they will look when printed, choose the [File] Print Preview command. To scroll to the next or preceding page, click the up or the down arrow in the scroll bar or click in the scroll bar above or below the scroll box. To move more quickly to a page farther from the present page, drag the scroll box. A document displayed in Print Preview is reduced, and you cannot edit it. To edit documents in their final, printed form, choose the [Document] Page View command.

You can move certain elements in Print Preview by using the icons on the left side of the window. From top to bottom the icons are

Page number icon Click to insert automatic page numbers in the document. The pointer changes to the numeral 1 when you click the icon. Drag the pointer to where you want the page number and click. To position page numbers at the upper-right corner of the page, double-click the page number icon.

Margins icon Displays margins, page breaks, and lines around page numbers, headers, footers, and positioned paragraphs. After clicking the icon, you can move these items by dragging them. For example, to change the margins, click the margins icon, click the margin handle (the box at the end of the margin line) of the margin you want to move, and drag the line to the new location. As you drag, Word displays the unit of measurement at the top of the window.

One page/Two page icon Click to alternate between displaying one and two pages at a time.

Printer icon Check to display the Print dialog box. To print the document, select the options you want from the dialog box and click the OK button.

To return to the view you left when you chose Print Preview (either Galley View or Page View), click Cancel. If you were in Galley View and want to see Page View, click the Page View button.

See also: Formatting sections, Galley View, Page View

Product support

Microsoft offers telephone support for Microsoft Word owners. Call (206) 454-2030. When you hear the automated voice instruction, dial 4 for the direct line for Macintosh Word assistance. Hours are 6:00 A.M. to 6:00 P.M. Pacific Standard Time (9:00 A.M. to 9:00 P.M. Eastern Standard Time).

QuickSwitch   *Command-comma (,)*

If you are running Apple's MultiFinder, you can use the QuickSwitch feature to link and update information shared among Word and the following programs: Microsoft Excel, SuperPaint 1.1 MS (the application supplied on the Microsoft Word Utilities disk), MacPaint, MacDraw, or any other application that supports QuickSwitch. For example, last month you might have copied a portion of a Microsoft Excel worksheet into a Word document. In the last week, you might have changed the Microsoft Excel worksheet. With QuickSwitch, you can update the portion of the worksheet in the Word document without recopying and pasting.

Linking the information

To link information in Microsoft Excel 1.5 and later and in SuperPaint 1.1 MS, choose Word's [Edit] Paste Link command instead of its [Edit] Paste command the first time you copy information from one of these programs to Word. First select the information in Microsoft Excel or SuperPaint and choose the application's [Edit] Copy command. Use MultiFinder to switch to Word, position the insertion point where you want to paste the information in the document, and choose Word's [Edit] Paste Link command.

When you paste with the [Edit] Paste Link command, Word inserts a hidden text identifier that specifies the source of the linked information. The identifier paragraph has the format *program!filename!area*. With Microsoft Excel versions 1.03, 1.04, and 1.06, you must type this identifier paragraph yourself. Copy the information from Microsoft Excel and paste it into Word as you normally would. Then type the identifier paragraph in the format *Excel!*filename*!RxCy:RxCy* at the beginning of the pasted information, where *filename* is the name of the Microsoft Excel worksheet and $RxCy:RxCy$ refers to the cell range of the information on the worksheet. You can also specify a name if the cell range has one.

In MacPaint and MacDraw, you do not have to use the [Edit] Paste Link command to link information. Simply copy and paste a graphic into your Word document by copying it to the Clipboard from MacPaint or MacDraw and then pasting it using the [Edit] Paste command in Word. When you want to update the graphic, Word switches to MacDraw or MacPaint, where you can make changes.

Updating the information

With Word's [Edit] Update Link command, you quickly transfer to Word information that has already been updated in another program.

To update linked information from Microsoft Excel 1.5 and later or from SuperPaint 1.1 MS, select the information in Word and choose Word's [Edit] Update Link command. Word starts the other application, opens the appropriate file, and transfers the updated information to the Word document.

To update a MacPaint or MacDraw graphic that you've already copied into Word, start the graphics application, open a new file, and switch to Word. Open the file that contains the graphic you want to change, select the graphic, and choose the [Edit] Update Link command. Word switches to the graphics application and pastes a copy of the graphic into the new file. After modifying the graphic, switch back to Word by pressing Command-comma (,). The new graphic replaces the graphic in the Word document.

Editing the information

With Word's [Edit] Edit Link command, you can quickly switch from Word to another program, edit the information at its source, and transfer the edited information back to Word.

To edit information in Microsoft Excel 1.5 and later or in SuperPaint 1.1 MS, select the information in Word that you want to edit, hold down the Shift key, and choose the [Edit] Edit Link (QuickSwitch) command. Word starts the other application and opens the appropriate file. Edit the information in Microsoft Excel or in SuperPaint and press Command-comma (,) to return to Word. The modified information replaces the old information in the Word document.

To edit information in applications other than Microsoft Excel 1.5 or SuperPaint 1.1 MS, start the other application and then switch to Word. Select the information you want to edit and choose the [Edit] Edit Link command. Word opens the appropriate file in the other application. Edit the information there and press Command-comma (,) to return to Word and transfer the updated information.

See also: MultiFinder

Quitting Word

To end a Word session, choose the [File] Quit command. If you haven't saved the changes you've made to a document, a glossary, or a spelling dictionary, Word asks whether you want to save your changes. Click the Yes button to save your changes; click the No button to discard the changes you've made since the last time you saved. If you haven't yet named a document, Word opens the Save As dialog box. Type a name for the document and click the Save button.

Word saves changes you've made in the [Edit] Preferences command and in the [Format] Document, Define Styles, and Section commands. These changes are stored in the Word Settings (4) file in the System folder. Word also saves any information that is stored on the Clipboard.

See also: Clipboard, Saving a document, Word Settings (4) file

Quotation marks

To insert typeset-quality quotation marks (" " or ' ') in your document whenever you press the quotation mark key (" or '), choose the [Edit] Preferences command, click the "Smart" Quotes option, and click OK. Word determines whether to insert an opening quotation mark (" or ') or a closing quotation mark (" or ') when you type.

You can also insert typeset-quality quotation marks with the following key combinations. For " type *Option-[*; for " type *Shift-Option-[*; for ' type *Option-]*; and for ' type *Shift-Option-]*.

Receiving mail

See: Mail

Redefining a style

Redefining a style means changing its formatting instructions. Every paragraph in the document to which that style has been applied then takes on the new formats. You can redefine a style with the ruler or with the [Format] Define Styles command.

With the ruler

Use the ruler method to quickly add or subtract formats for a style. By adding or subtracting the formats for a paragraph that already has a style close to the one you want, you can redefine the style "by example." For instance, you might want to change the style *heading* from Italic, 18 point Geneva, and Centered to Bold Italic, 18 point Geneva, and Centered.

To redefine a style with the ruler, add or subtract formats for a paragraph that has the style you want to redefine. In our example, you would select the paragraph and then choose the [Format] Bold command. Then choose the [Format] Show Ruler command to display the ruler, choose the name of the style from the style box (*heading* in our example), click the Redefine the style based on selection option, and click OK. Every paragraph with the style you just redefined will be modified.

If you made a mistake in redefining the style and want to change your paragraph back to the original style, choose the Reapply the style to the selection option after choosing the style name from the ruler, and then click OK. Word returns the paragraph to its original formats and leaves the style unchanged.

Comments
If you've added character formats to a paragraph (but not to the style) and then you decide you liked it better before you made the changes, reset the paragraph by selecting it and choosing the [Format] Plain for Style command or by pressing Command-Shift-Spacebar.

With the [Format] Define Styles command
Use the [Format] Define Styles command to redefine more than one style at a time or to change the Based on: style or the style you specified in the Next Style: box. Choose the [Format] Define Styles command and select the style you want to change from the list box. With the Define Styles dialog box still open, add or subtract formats by choosing commands from the Format and Font menus and by changing settings on the ruler. After checking the formatting instructions in the dialog box to be sure they include the changes you want, click the Define button to redefine the style or click the Apply button to redefine the style and apply it to selected text. The dialog box remains open so that you can redefine another style. To redefine the style, apply the style to text, and close the dialog box, you simply click OK.

See also: Applying a style, Defining a style, Next style, Styles, Style sheets

Repaginating

See: Page breaks

Repeating commands   *Command-A*

To repeat the last command and any changes to options in its dialog box or to repeat the last text you typed, choose the [Edit] Again command. For example, if you choose the [Format] Paragraph command to change line spacing, add a border, and change the indents for a paragraph, you can quickly format another paragraph in the same way by choosing the [Edit] Again command as your next action. The name of the Again command changes to reflect the last action you performed; for example, Format Again, or Edit Again.

Note that some commands cannot be repeated with the [Edit] Again command. When this is the case for a command you've chosen, the [Edit] Again command will be disabled and will appear dimmed in the Edit menu. The [Utilities] Find command is one command that can't be repeated by using [Edit] Again. To repeat the [Utilities] Find command, you have to use the [Utilities] Find Again command (Command-Option-A).

See also: Searching and replacing

Repeating text

See: Glossary

Ruler

The ruler is the horizontal scale (at the top of the document window) that controls paragraph formatting and tab stops. To display the ruler, choose the [Format] Show Ruler command.

The ruler displays the unit of measurement you've chosen in the [Edit] Preferences dialog box. To change the unit of measurement, choose the [Edit] Preferences command, choose a different unit of measurement from the Default Measure: list, and click OK.

To change the ruler settings for a paragraph or for a number of paragraphs, select the paragraph(s) or place the insertion point within a paragraph, display the ruler, and choose from the following icons (listed in left-to-right order):

Indent markers Change the indents for selected paragraphs by dragging the markers to change the indents.

Style selection box Choose a style from the style box in the same way you choose a command from a menu.

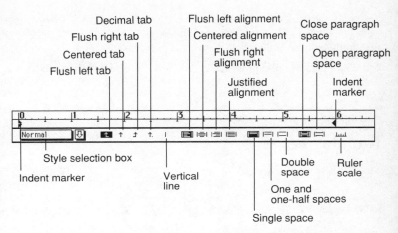

Flush left, centered, flush right, and decimal aligned tabs Choose from
among the tab icons to set tab stops. Default tab stops are set at 0.5-
inch intervals. To specify other tab stops to align text flush left, centered, or flush right at a tab or to align numbers with decimal points at
a tab, click the icon you want and then click beneath the measurement
on the ruler where you want the tab stop. If you have set a decimal tab
stop, pressing Tab before a number moves the decimal point in the
number to the decimal tab stop.

Vertical line Click the icon and then click below a measurement on the
ruler. Word draws a vertical line the height of the selected paragraph
within the paragraph at the horizontal position specified by the measurement you've chosen.

Flush left, centered, flush right, justified alignment Click the type of
alignment you want.

Single space, one and one-half spaces, double space Click the type of
line spacing you want.

Close paragraph space, open paragraph space Click the close space
icon to remove a 12-point line space above a selected paragraph. Click
the open space icon to add 12 points above a selected paragraph.

Ruler scale Click to display one of three views (scales) of the ruler.
Normal scale displays tabs and indents, and the 0 mark is at the left
column boundary of the selected paragraph. Normal scale is the scale
that first appears when you choose [Format] Show Ruler. Page scale
displays text margins, and the 0 mark is at the left edge of the page.
Table scale displays table columns and the table's column boundaries
when the insertion point is in a table.

To display the ruler whenever you open a document window, choose [Edit] Commands, select Open Documents with Ruler from the list box, and click the Do button.

See also: Aligning paragraphs, Customizing Word, Defining a style, Tabs

Running heads

See: Headers and footers

Saving a document

To save a document on disk for the first time, choose the [File] Save As command, type a name for the document, and click Save. Document names can be any combination of characters excluding the colon (:). Word always saves the document on the current disk. To save the document on a different disk, click Drive to change disks or click Eject to eject the current disk, replace it with another, and click Save.

As you make changes to a document, save the document on disk every 10 to 15 minutes to ensure that you don't lose information because of a power failure or a mechanical problem. To save changes to a document that you have already saved at least once, choose the [File] Save command.

To save a revised version of a document that you have already saved at least once, choose the [File] Save As command, type a new name for the document, and click Save. This will give you two versions of the same document—the original with the first name and the revised document with the second name.

To make a backup copy of a document, choose the [File] Save As command, type a name for the document, click the Make Backup option, and click Save. Word names the document *Backup of filename*. From now on when you save this document, Word saves the previous version in *Backup of filename*, giving you two versions—one that contains the most recent editing changes and one that contains your document before it was last edited.

The Fast Save option in the Save As dialog box is the default option for most document saves (except when you have chosen Make Backup). The Fast Save option speeds up the editing and saving of documents by keeping a list in Random Access Memory (RAM) of the edits you make to a document instead of changing the base document each time you make editing changes and save them. Don't turn this option off unless you are transferring a Word document to another program—such as Aldus PageMaker—that requires you to do a full save.

Saving in different formats

To save a document in a different file format, choose the [File] Save As command, type a name for the document, and click the File Format button. Choose from among the options listed below, click Format, and then click Save.

Normal Saves the document in standard Microsoft Word format.

Text Only Saves the document in ASCII (American Standard Code for Information Interchange) format. Files saved in ASCII format contain text only—no formatting or line breaks.

Text Only with Line Breaks Saves the document in ASCII format, which contains text only, but with a return character at the end of each line.

Microsoft Word 1.0/Microsoft Works Saves the document in a format that can be read by Microsoft Word 1 and Microsoft Works. If you choose this option, the document's formatting for tables, positioned paragraphs, outlining levels, styles, color, and hidden text will not be transferred.

Microsoft Word 3.0/Microsoft Write Saves the document in a format that can be read by Microsoft Word 3 and Microsoft Write. The document's formats for tables, positioned paragraphs, and color will not be transferred.

Microsoft Word MS-DOS Saves the document in a format that can be read by Word for IBM PCs and compatibles. Some features of the document, such as tables and outlining levels, might not be transferable. Use this option to save files to be read by Microsoft Word versions 4 and earlier for IBM PCs and compatibles.

MacWrite Saves the document in a format that can be read by Mac-Write. Features such as tables, outlining levels, and styles will not be transferred.

Interchange Format (RTF) Saves the document in a special Microsoft word-processing format that converts Word formatting to ASCII so that the document can be read by programs that are able to read RTF (Rich Text Format). If you are transferring files between Macintosh Word and PC Word, you can preserve the formatting of the Macintosh Word files by using the DCA (Document Content Architecture) conversion program that comes with your Macintosh Word 4 software. To convert a Macintosh Word document to PC Word (DCA) format, choose the [File] Save As command and click File Format. Choose Interchange Format (RTF), click OK, and then click Save. Quit Word, insert the Word Utilities disk into a drive if you don't have the utilities on hard disk, and double-click the DCA Conversion icon. Choose the [File] Open command, select the document you want to convert, type a name for the converted document, and click Convert. Use this option for saving files to be read by Microsoft Word 5 or Microsoft Works 2 for the PC.

Default Format for File Makes the format you've selected for saving documents the default format for the current Word session.

Scrapbook

The Scrapbook is a temporary holding place in which you can store as many as 256 items. To transfer part of a Word document to the Scrapbook, select the text you want to transfer and choose the [Edit] Cut or Copy command to transfer the item onto the Clipboard. Then choose the [Apple] Scrapbook command and choose the Paste command from the Scrapbook's Edit menu. To close the Scrapbook, click the close box or click anywhere outside the Scrapbook's window.

To paste an item from the Scrapbook into a document, position the insertion point where you want the item in the document and choose the [Apple] Scrapbook command. Scroll to find the item you want, choose the [Edit] Copy command, click outside the Scrapbook window, and choose the [Edit] Paste command.

To move the Scrapbook window, drag its title bar.

See also: Clipboard, Copying text, Moving text

Scrolling

Use the horizontal and vertical scroll bars to move around in a document. Scrolling works the same way in Galley View and Page View but differently in Print Preview.

In Galley View and Page View

To scroll up or down line by line through a document, click the up or down arrow at each end of the vertical scroll bar. To scroll up or down one screen at a time, click above or below the scroll box in the vertical scroll bar. To scroll to a particular place in a document, drag the scroll box to the approximate position in the vertical scroll bar. (Dragging the scroll box to the bottom of the bar takes you to the end of the document.) As you drag the scroll box within the vertical scroll bar, the lower-left corner of the window displays the current page number if your document has been paginated. To scroll to the next or previous page in Page View, click the page forward or page back icon.

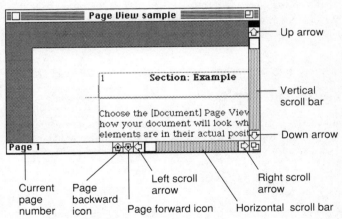

To scroll right or left, follow the procedures above using the right or left arrow and the scroll box of the horizontal scroll bar. To scroll to the left of the left margin (if you have a negative, or hanging, indent), hold down the Shift key as you click the left scroll arrow.

To move to a specific page, choose the [Utilities] Go To command, type the page number, and click OK. To move to the previous selection or to the previous position of the insertion point, choose the [Utilities] Go Back command.

To speed up scrolling in a document that contains graphics, choose the [Edit] Preferences command, check Use Picture Placeholders, and click OK. Word inserts gray rectangles in place of the graphics in Galley View and Page View. When you choose the [File] Print Preview command or print the document, Word displays or prints the graphics.

To quickly scroll through a long document, choose the [Document] Outlining command and collapse (hide) subheadings until you see the heading for the section to which you want to move. Select the heading and scroll down until the heading is at the top of the window and choose the [Document] Outlining command again to return to Galley View. Word will scroll to the heading and select the heading and its accompanying text.

In Print Preview

To switch to Print Preview, choose the [File] Print Preview command.

To scroll to the next or previous page, click the up or down arrow or click above or below the scroll box in the vertical scroll bar. When you are viewing two pages at a time, Word "flips" the pages so that the right page moves to the left and the new page comes into view on the right.

Searching and replacing

Word can search for text, search for character or paragraph formats, or search for text and replace it with other text. You can use wildcard symbols and special symbols in both the search text and the replace text.

Searching for text

To search your document for the next occurrence of specific text, position the insertion point where you want to start the search, choose the [Utilities] Find command, and type the text you want to find. Click Whole Word to search only for entire words containing the text (so that Word finds *bus* but not *business*), and click Match Upper/Lowercase to search only for words that duplicate the case of the search text. Then click Start Search. To find the next occurrence of the text while the Find dialog box is still open, click the Find Next button. To find the next occurrence after you've closed the Find dialog box, choose the [Utilities] Find Again command.

Searching for character or paragraph formats

To search your document for a specific format, select a character or a paragraph with the format you want to look for and press Command-Option-R. To search for the next occurrence of the format, choose the [Utilities] Find Again command.

Searching for and replacing text

To search for and replace text throughout an entire document, position the insertion point at the beginning of the document. To search and replace within a selection, select the text first. Then choose the [Utilities] Change command, type the text you want to change in the Find What: box, and type the new text in the Change To: box. Click Whole Word to replace only entire words containing the Find What: text, and click Match Upper/Lowercase to search only for words that duplicate the case of the search text. To review and approve each change, click the Start Search button. Click Change to change the selected text or No Change to leave the text unchanged. To replace all occurrences of the text without reviewing each instance, click Change All or Change Selection.

Wildcard (?) and special symbols

With either the Find or the Change command, you can use the wildcard symbol (?) in the Find What: box to search for one or more characters accompanied by any character in the wildcard position. For example, type *M?.* to find Mr. or Ms. You cannot use the wildcard (?) in the Change To: box.

To search for or to search for and replace special characters, use the following symbols in either the Find What: box or the Change To: box. Note that you can combine these symbols with other text.

Type	To find
^?	A question mark
^w	A white space
^t	A tab character
^p	A paragraph mark
^n	An end-of-line mark
^-	An optional hyphen
^~	A nonbreaking hyphen
^s	A nonbreaking space
^d	A section mark or page break
^\	A formula character
^^	A caret (^) symbol
^1	A graphic
^5	A footnote reference mark

Comments

To replace entire paragraphs of text, copy the new paragraphs onto the Clipboard and choose the [Utilities] Change command. Type the text you want to search for in the Find What: box and type ^c in the Change To: box. Word replaces the occurrences of the text you've typed with the contents of the Clipboard.

Section formatting

See: Formatting sections

Selecting

In Galley View and Page View, you can select text; columns, rows, and cells in a table; columns that are not part of a table; and graphic frames.

Text

To select text, position the insertion point where you want the selection to begin, click, and then drag to where you want the selection to end. If you select text near the bottom of the window, Word scrolls the text as you select. To select a large portion of text that extends over many windows, position the insertion point where you want the selection to begin, scroll to the page in which your selection ends, and then hold down the Shift key and click at the end of the selection.

You can also use these shortcuts for selecting text: To select a line, position the pointer at the far left of the line and click; to select an entire paragraph, position the pointer at the far left of the paragraph and double-click. Notice that when you place the pointer at the far left, it changes from a left-pointing arrow or an I-beam to a right-pointing arrow. To select a word, position the insertion point anywhere inside the word and double-click. To select a sentence, position the insertion point anywhere in the sentence, press the Command key, and click.

Table columns, rows, and cells

To select a column in a table, hold down the Option key and click anywhere in the column. To select a row in a table, double-click to the left of any cell in the row you want to select. To select a cell, click to the left of the cell. To select the entire table, hold down the Option key and double-click anywhere in the table.

To select text within a table, follow the procedures above for selecting text. Note that the shortcuts for selecting a line or a paragraph don't work in a table.

Nontable columns

To select columns that are not part of a table (data separated by tabs, for example), hold down the Option key and drag from the upper-left corner of the column to the lower-right corner.

Graphics

To select a graphic, click inside the graphic frame or drag over the graphic. A graphic's frame is selected when the frame's sizing handles (three black squares) are visible.

See also: Galley View, Graphics, Page View, Tables

Sending mail

See: Mail

Side-by-side paragraphs

See: Columns, Tables

Sizing windows

See: Windows

"Smart" quotes

See: Quotation marks

Sorting

To sort paragraphs, lines, or columns in ascending order (lowest to highest; a–z), select the text you want to sort and choose the [Utilities] Sort command. To sort in descending order (highest to lowest; z–a), select the text you want to sort and hold down the Shift key while choosing the [Utilities] Sort command. Word bases its sorts on the first character of each paragraph, line, or column.

To specify a table column or a tabular column on which to base a sort, select the column (Option-click in a table or Option-drag in tabular text) and choose the [Utilities] Sort command. To use more than one column as references for sorting the rows of a table, select all the columns you want to have an effect on the sort and choose the [Utilities] Sort command. Word first sorts rows according to values in the leftmost column in the selection; then, if values in the first column are equal, Word sorts those rows according to values in the next column, and so on. In tables, Word reorders rows as it sorts. In tabular text, Word reorders lines and paragraphs.

To sort an entire document, position the insertion point anywhere in the document and choose the [Utilities] Sort command. If the document includes a table, Word reorders the table according to the first cell in each row.

When Word sorts data copied from another program such as Microsoft Excel, it sorts by the first field if the fields are separated by commas. If the fields are separated by tabs, you can select the column (Option-drag) on which you want Word to base the sort.

Comments
A quick way to reorganize many paragraphs of text is to type to the left of each paragraph the number for the new sequence, select the paragraphs, and choose the [Utilities] Sort command. You can then delete the sequence numbers.

See also: Selecting, Tables, Tabs

Spell checking

To check the spelling of words in an entire document, position the insertion point at the beginning of the document and choose the [Utilities] Spelling command. If the file MS Dictionary is not on one of the current disks, Word asks you to locate the file. After inserting in a drive the disk that contains the MS Dictionary (if necessary), click Start Check to begin the spell checking.

Word matches words to the spellings in the MS Dictionary and displays a misspelled word or a proper name next to Unknown Word. To change the word, either type the correct spelling in the Change To: box and click Change or click Suggest to see a list of alternatives. To change the word to one of the suggested words, select the alternative and click Change. To check the spelling of a word you've just typed in the Change To: box, click the checkmark button. To leave the unknown word as is, click No Change. To continue checking the rest of the document, click Continue Check.

If you clicked No Change for an unknown word, Word subsequently accepts the word that was previously unknown. Word keeps a list of words that you've implied were spelled correctly when you clicked No Change, maintaining this list until you end the session. In order to once again check the spelling of every word in your document, reset this list by pressing the Shift key and choosing the [Utilities] Reset Spelling command.

You can add to the MS Dictionary so that when you do a spell check in a new session, Word doesn't flag proper names or words that have unusual spellings. Click the plus button when Word displays in the Spelling dialog box the word you want to add to the MS Dictionary. Word also creates a dictionary called User1 to which you can add words that you don't want to add to the MS Dictionary. You could use the User1 dictionary to store words specific to one type of document. For example, documents about computers will undoubtedly contain jargon that is unique to the computer industry. You can store these words in a user dictionary such as User1 for use with any document. To add words to User1, select User1 in the Open Dictionaries list box and then click the plus button. To delete a word from a dictionary, select the dictionary from the Open Dictionaries: box and click the minus button.

You can create other dictionaries (User2, User3, and so on) by choosing the [File] New command while the Spelling dialog box is open. When you check the spelling in your document, Word always checks MS Dictionary and any user dictionaries that are open. To open other dictionaries, choose the [File] Open command while the Spelling dialog box is open and double-click the name of the dictionary you want to use.

Give your user dictionaries descriptive names. To rename a user dictionary, select it from the Open Dictionaries box, choose the [File]

Save As command, type a new name for the dictionary, and click Save. To close a dictionary you aren't using, select the dictionary from the Open Dictionaries box and choose the [File] Close command.

When you quit the program, Word stores in the current configuration file (Word Settings (4) or one of your own) a list of the dictionaries you used. The next time you use Word and the Spelling command, Word opens those dictionaries.

Comments
To check spelling in hidden text, be sure to choose the [Edit] Preferences command and check the Show Hidden Text option.

Starting Word

By double-clicking different icons in the Finder, you can start the Word program only or you can start Word and open documents:

To start	Do this
The Word program	Double-click the Microsoft Word icon
The Word program and open one document	Double-click the document icon
The Word program and many documents	Select all the documents, and then double-click one of the documents
A particular customized version of Word	Double-click the Settings file you want to use

The first time you start Word, you must personalize your copy of the program by typing your name (and your company's name, if applicable) in a special dialog box. The first time you start the program, be sure to choose the [Edit] Full Menus command to display all Word commands.

See also: Customizing Word, Opening a document

Styles

A style is a group of character and paragraph formats to which you give a name. By using styles, you can quickly format a document. For example, you might define a style called *major heading* that has the formats Geneva, 18 point, and hairline border above. Whenever you want a paragraph to have these formats, you apply the style *major heading*. Instead of applying each format individually, you apply the style only once. Later, you might decide that 18-point type is too small for your major headings. Instead of searching through your entire document and changing each major heading to 24-point type, you can make a one-time change to the formatting instructions for the style *major heading* so that all the major headings in the document will be reformatted.

As you type text in a new document, the text is assigned the automatic style *Normal* (New York, 12 point, and flush left). Word adds other automatic styles to the document's style sheet (list of styles) as you add certain elements to your document (headers, footers, page numbers, and so on). The automatic styles are those defined by Word. You can redefine an automatic style as you would any other style. For example, if you want the font for all your documents to be Chicago instead of New York, you can redefine the style *Normal*.

The styles you create for one document can also be used with other documents. If your company uses a standard format for memos, you can distribute the same style sheet to all employees so that they have the formats they need at their fingertips.

See also: Applying a style, Automatic styles, Defining a style, Next style, Redefining a style, Style sheets

Style sheets

A style sheet is a list of all styles—groups of character and paragraph formats—for a document. A style sheet can contain as many as 221 styles. To display a document's style sheet, choose the [File] Open command to open the document and choose either the [Format] Styles command or the [Format] Show Ruler command and click the arrow to the right of the style selection box. To print the style sheet for your document, choose the [Format] Define Styles command and with the dialog box still open, choose the [File] Print command.

If you haven't defined styles for the document, the style sheet contains one default style: the automatic style called *Normal* (New York, 12 point, and flush left). Word applies the *Normal* style to all text you type. As you add elements such as headers, footers, and footnotes to your document, Word adds the automatic styles for those elements to the style sheet.

Changing the default style sheet

If you want every new document to contain certain styles, you can change the default style sheet. First, either open the document that contains the styles you want or define the styles you want in your document. Then choose the [Format] Define Styles command and select the style you want to add to the default style sheet. Click the Set Default button and click Yes. Select another style you want to add and repeat the procedure. To delete a style from the default style sheet, choose the [Format] Define Styles command, select the style, choose the [Edit] Cut command, and click OK. When you are satisfied with the new default style sheet, click OK in the Define Styles dialog box.

The default style sheet is saved in the Word Settings (4) file. To return this style sheet to its original form, delete the Word Settings (4) file from the System disk (or from the System folder if it is on your hard disk). When you restart Word, a settings file that contains the original default settings (*Normal* style and the other automatic styles) is created.

Using a style sheet with another document

To use a style sheet with another document, choose the [File] Open command, open the document you want to receive the style sheet, and choose the [Format] Define Styles command. With the dialog box still open, choose the [File] Open command and double-click the name of the document that contains the style sheet you want to use. Word copies the styles to the open document. If the open document already contains styles, Word combines the two style sheets. If two styles have the same name, Word creates one style with that name using the formatting from the incoming style.

See also: Applying a style, Automatic styles, Defining a style, Next style, Redefining a style, Styles, Word Settings (4) file

Subtracting

See: Math

Symbols

To display symbols on the screen such as dots for spaces, arrows for tabs, ¶ for paragraph marks, and end-of-cell marks in tables, choose the [Edit] Show ¶ command.

See also: Formulas

Table of contents

You create a table of contents for a document by using existing headings from a document's outline or by inserting table of contents codes in your document. Word adds the headings or entries to the table of contents, inserts leader tabs (.........) and page numbers, and copies the table of contents to the beginning of your document (separated from the main text by a section mark).

Using outline headings

To compile a table of contents from the headings of your outline, choose the [Utilities] Table of Contents command and click Outline in the Collect box. Type the levels of heading you want to be included in the table of contents, and click the Start button.

Note that if you do not use the [Document] Outlining command to organize your document, you can still use the outline method to create a table of contents if you use the automatic styles *heading 1*, *heading 2*, and so on, as the styles of the headings in your document. When you use these automatic styles, Word builds an outline for you.

Inserting table of contents codes

To insert a table of contents code, select the text you want to be included in the table of contents, choose the [Edit] Preferences command, and be sure that Show Hidden Text is chosen. Then choose the [Document] Insert TOC Entry command. Word inserts the code .c. before the text and a semicolon (;) after the text. If the text is at the end of a paragraph, Word uses the paragraph mark as the ending code and does not insert a semicolon. Use this method for including text that is already in your document in the table of contents. For example,

.c.Overview of the Roman Government;

To type a new table of contents entry, choose the [Document] Insert TOC Entry command and then type the entry between the .c. code and the semicolon. Word formats as hidden text the codes and formats as well as the text you type. Use this method for inserting table of contents entries that are not included as text in your document. For example,

.c.The Forum;

To indicate subentries and include a leader tab and page number for all levels, position the insertion point between the c and the last period in the .c. code and type a number from 1 through 9 to designate a level. For example, type

.c1.Overview of the Roman Government;.c2.The Forum;

to produce

Overview of the Roman Government..1
        The Forum 2

To indicate subentries and include a leader tab and page number for the last level only, type all the entries within the same .c. code and separate them with colons. For example, type

.c.Overview of the Roman Government:The Forum;

to produce

Overview of the Roman Government
        The Forum 2

If you want to have part of the text between the .c. and the semicolon printed with the document, select the text and remove the hidden format by choosing the [Format] Plain Text command.

Compiling the table of contents

To compile the table of contents when you have used the .c. code throughout your document, choose the [Utilities] Table of Contents command and click .C. Paragraphs in the Collect box. Type the levels of entry you want to be included in the table of contents and click the Start button.

Levels in the table of contents are formatted with the automatic styles *toc1* through *toc9*. You can change the formats of the levels by redefining the automatic styles.

See also: Hidden text, Linking documents, Redefining a style

Tables

To create text in multiple or side-by-side columns, position the insertion point where you want the columns and choose the [Document] Insert Table command. Type the number of columns and the number of rows you want and click the OK button. Word divides the text area width evenly among the columns. To see the gridlines that separate rows and columns and the marks that designate the ends of cells, choose the [Edit] Show ¶ command. Within each cell in a table, you can type or copy as many paragraphs as you want. To type text into a table cell, position the insertion point before the end-of-cell mark (a small dot) and type. As you type, text within the cell wraps to the next line when necessary and Word adjusts the height of the entire row. To move from cell to cell, press Tab or Shift-Tab.

Formatting tables

Format the text within a cell as you would text within a paragraph: Change the font and font size and add bold, italic, or any other character or paragraph formats.

To use the ruler to format a table, alternate between two ruler scales: normal scale and table scale. In normal scale, the 0 mark corresponds to the left edge of the current column. You can set indents, tabs, alignment, and spacing for the current paragraph in a cell. To see normal scale, position the insertion point in one of the table's cells and choose the [Format] Show Ruler command.

In table scale, the 0 mark corresponds to the left edge of the table and small T icons mark each column boundary. You can set the boundaries of the table in this scale. To see table scale, click the scale icon (the far right icon) on the ruler.

To change column boundaries in table scale, select the rows for the column boundaries you want to change (press Option and double-click if you want to select the entire table) and drag the T icons on the ruler.

To drag the T icons individually, hold down the Shift key while you drag. To switch back to normal scale, click the scale icon twice.

To change column boundaries using the [Format] Cells command, select the cells or columns you want to change, choose the [Format] Cells command, and type a width in the Width of Column: box. Click Selection to change the width for only the selected cells or click Whole Table to change the width for the entire column, and click OK.

To change row alignment, select the rows, choose the [Format] Cells command, and click the Left, Center, or Right Align Rows option. Click Selection to align only the selected rows or click Whole Table to align all rows in the table, and click OK.

To specify the minimum row height, select the rows, choose the [Format] Cells command, type a number of points in the Minimum Row Height: box, and click OK.

To put borders around cells, select the cells, choose the [Format] Cells command, and click the Borders button. Choose the border style you want, click in the border guides to add the borders, and click OK.

To insert a tab stop into a table cell, press Option-Tab. If you insert a decimal tab in a cell, Word will move to the decimal place when you press Tab to move to that cell.

Editing tables

To insert a row or column in a table, position the insertion point in the row below or in the column to the right of where you want the new row or column. Choose the [Edit] Table command, click Row or Column, and click Insert. To insert a few cells at a time, select an area of cells equal in size to the area you want to insert and choose the [Edit] Table command. Click Horizontally to shift the selected cells to the right or click Vertically to shift the cells down, and click Insert. The selected cells will be moved right or down, and new cells will be inserted in the resulting space.

To insert a row at the end of a table, position the insertion point at the end of the table's last cell and press the Tab key.

To delete a row or column from a table, select the row or column and choose the [Edit] Table command. Click Row or Column, and click Delete. To delete a few cells, select the cells you want to delete and choose the [Edit] Table command. Click Selection, or click Horizontally to shift cells left or Vertically to shift cells up, and click the Delete button. The selected cells will be deleted, and either the cells to the right of the selection will be moved left to fill the position or the cells below the selection will be moved up to take the place of the deleted cells.

To merge two or more cells into one, select the cells, choose the [Edit] Table command, and click Merge Cells. You can merge cells only horizontally, across rows. To split a merged cell, select the cell, choose the [Edit] Table command, and click Split Cell.

To copy or move cells, use the [Edit] Copy, Cut, and Paste commands as you do for copying or moving paragraphs. For example, to move cells from one place to another within the table, select the cells including the end-of-cell marks. Choose the [Edit] Cut command, select an area the same size as the cells, and choose the [Edit] Paste command. The size of the paste area must be the same size as the cells you are copying or moving.

Converting text to table/table to text

To convert regular text into a table, select the text and choose the [Document] Insert Table command. Select Paragraphs, Tab Delimited, Comma Delimited, or Side By Side Only from among the Convert From options to specify what will indicate the end of one cell and the beginning of another; then be sure that the number of columns and rows is correct and click OK.

To convert rows in a table to text, select the rows you want to convert and choose the [Document] Table to Text command. Select Paragraphs, Tab delimited, or Comma delimited to specify the separator between elements and click OK.

See also: Borders, Columns

Tabs

Use tab stops to position text within single lines or within a column in a table. To set up multiple columns, insert a table in your document. You can insert tab stops with either the ruler or the [Format] Paragraph command.

Tabs and the ruler

To insert tabs with the ruler, choose the [Format] Show Ruler command and select the paragraphs for which you want to set tabs. Click the icon for one of the following tabs (from left to right on the ruler),

and click on the ruler below the measurement at which you want the
tab stop:

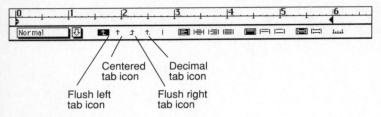

Flush left tab icon Aligns text flush left, to the right of the tab stop.

Centered tab icon Centers text on the tab stop.

Flush right tab icon Aligns text flush right, to the left of the tab stop.

Decimal tab icon Aligns decimal points of numbers at the tab stop.

To move a tab stop, drag the stop to the position on the ruler where
you want it.

To remove a tab stop with the ruler, select the paragraph that contains
the tab stop and drag the tab stop down and off the ruler.

Tabs and the [Format] Paragraph command

To insert tabs with the Paragraph command, select the paragraphs for
which you want to set tabs, choose the [Format] Paragraph command,
and click the Tabs button. Type the position at which you want to set
the tab, or click the position on the ruler, and then click the tab type
you want. Click the Set button, click OK to close the Tabs box, and
click OK to close the Paragraph dialog box.

To insert leader tabs (such as .... in a table of contents), select the
paragraph, choose the [Format] Paragraph command, and click the
Tabs button. Type the position at which you want to set the tab, or
click on the ruler, and then select a leader type. Click OK to close the
Tabs box and click OK again to close the Paragraph dialog box.

To remove a tab stop with the Paragraph command, select the paragraph that contains the tab stop you want to remove, choose the
[Format] Paragraph command, and click the Tabs button. In the Position: box type the position of the tab stop you want to delete or click
the tab on the ruler. Click Clear, click OK to close the Tabs box, and
click OK again to close the Paragraph dialog box.

Changing default tabs

To change the default tab stops (every ½ inch), choose the [Format] Document command, type the default measurement you want to use in the Default Tab Stops: box, and click OK. To change the default tab stops for all future documents, click Set Default and then click OK.

See also: Formatting paragraphs, Tables

Title page

To create a title page that doesn't contain a header, footer, or page number, type the text for the title page, insert a page break by pressing Shift-Enter, and position the insertion point above the page break. Choose the [Format] Section command, select First Page Special under Header/Footer, and click OK. Continue typing the rest of the document after the page break. To include headers or footers and page numbers for the rest of the document, choose the [Document] Open Header or Open Footer command, type the header or footer text, and click the page number icon. The title page will be unnumbered, and page numbers will begin with the numeral 2 on page 2.

To include special header or footer text or a special page number on the title page, follow the procedures above for setting up the title page. Then choose the [Document] Open First Header or Open First Footer command, type the header or footer text, and click the page number icon. The title page will have the special header, footer, or page number, and the rest of the document will have the header, footer, or page number you typed in the Open Header or Open Footer window.

To create an unnumbered title page followed by page 1, type the text for the title page, insert a section break by pressing Command-Enter, and position the insertion point above the section break. Choose the [Format] Section command, select First Page Special under Header/Footer, and click OK. Position the insertion point after the section break, choose the [Format] Section command, and select New Page from the Start: box. Check Restart at 1 under Page Number, click First Page Special to delete the check under Headers/Footers, and click OK. Then choose the [Document] Open Header or Open Footer command, type header or footer text, and add page numbers.

Typing text

Text you type is inserted at the insertion point. If you type when text is selected, what you type replaces the selection. Text you type is formatted in the style of the current paragraph. If you have not defined styles, text is in *Normal* style (12 point, New York, and flush left). When you reach the end of a line, text wraps to the next line.

Underlining

See: Formatting characters

Undoing

To undo your last action, choose the [Edit] Undo command. Many editing and formatting actions can be undone if you choose the [Edit] Undo command as the very next action. The name of the [Edit] Undo command changes depending on the most recent action. For example, if you just applied Bold to a heading, the name of the Undo command changes to Undo Formatting. If the most recent command cannot be undone, the Undo command changes to Can't Undo and is dimmed.

After you choose the [Edit] Undo command, the command name changes to Redo. If you change your mind about undoing an action, choose the [Edit] Redo command.

Wildcard symbol (?)

See: Searching and replacing

Windows

You can have up to 22 windows on the screen at once. To open a window to another document, choose the [File] Open command and double-click the document you want to open. To open another window to the same document, click in the document's window to make it the active window and choose the [Window] New Window command. Changes you make in one window are made in all other windows of that document.

Word positions the new window on top of other windows and adds the document name or the window name to the Window menu. Successive windows for the same document are numbered (for example, Report:1, Report:2). To move a window, position the pointer on the window's title bar and drag the window to a new position. To work in a different window, make the window active either by clicking in it or by choosing its name from the Window menu.

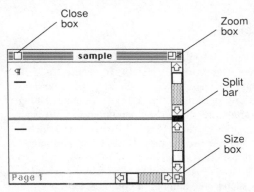

To size a window, drag the size box. To alternate between a full size window and a smaller size window, click the zoom box. The full size of a window depends on monitor size and on the page size you specified in the Page Setup dialog box.

To split a window (create panes), drag the black split bar from the top of the vertical scroll bar to where you want the window to be divided. You can scroll each pane of the window separately by using the scroll bars as you normally would. Each pane contains the entire document. To see a different view of a document (such as Page View or Outline View) in a pane of a split window, click the pane in which you want the different view and choose the appropriate command from the menu. (For example, choose the [Document] Page View command.) To return to a one-paned window, drag the black split bar to the top or bottom of the window.

To close a window, click the close box in the upper-left corner. If you've made unsaved changes and you close the last open window for a document, Word asks if you want to save the changes. Click Yes to save the changes. Click No to close the document without saving the changes.

See also: Opening a document, Scrolling

Word count

See: Counting

Word Settings (4) file

When you quit Word, a configuration file called Word Settings (4) is saved in the System folder. The Word Settings (4) file keeps track of the following settings and uses any changes to the settings as defaults the next time you start Word: options in the [Edit] Preferences dialog box such as unit of measurement; whether to open documents in Page View; full or short menus; hide or show ¶; [File] Print options such as the print hidden text option or printer quality; [File] Page Setup and [Format] Document options such as paper size and margins; styles you add and changes you make to *Normal* or to the other automatic styles; [Format] Section options such as the number of columns; any font you add to the Font menu; and finally, any changes you make using the [Edit] Commands command. Note that to add changes you've made in the Document, Section, and Define Styles dialog boxes to the Word Settings (4) file, you must click Set Default in the appropriate dialog box.

To reset the defaults to the original Microsoft settings, delete the Word Settings (4) file from your System folder. When you restart, Word creates a new Word Settings (4) file containing the original settings.

You can create and save your own configuration files by using the [Edit] Commands command to customize Word.

See also: Customizing Word

Zooming windows

See: Windows

Appendix:
The Keyboard

Keyboard command equivalents are listed on the Word menus to the right of the command names. Symbols on the menus refer to the following keys:

Symbol on menu	Key
⌘	Command
⇧	Shift
⬈	Option
⌄	Enter
▬	Spacebar

The rest of this appendix provides keyboard equivalents for performing these tasks: choosing commands, working in a dialog box, moving, scrolling, selecting, editing, formatting, outlining, working in Page View, and using the extended keyboard.

Note: Keyboards covered here include those for the Macintosh Plus and the Macintosh SE and the Macintosh II Extended Keyboard. This appendix does not include keys for the original Macintosh keyboard.

Choosing commands

To choose commands with the keyboard, use either the keyboard command equivalents listed on the menus or the following techniques:

To	Press
Activate menu bar	Command-Tab or the period on the numeric keypad
Specify which menu to pull down	First letter of the menu name or the left or right arrow key
Choose command in that menu	First letter of the command name, then Return or Enter

Working in a dialog box

To	Press
Move to next text box	Tab
Move to previous text box	Shift-Tab
Scroll a list box	Up or down arrow
Move to next group of options	Right arrow
Move to previous group of options	Left arrow
Move to next option	Command-Tab
Move to previous option	Shift-Command-Tab
Select an option	Command-Spacebar
Pull down a list box	Command-Spacebar
Select an option when in a pull-down list box	Return or Enter
Open a folder	Command-Down arrow
Close a folder	Command-Up arrow
Click OK	Return or Enter
Click Cancel	Command-period (.)

Moving, scrolling, and selecting

To move	Press
Up one line	Up arrow
Down one line	Down arrow
Left one character	Left arrow
Right one character	Right arrow
To previous word	Command-4 (keypad)
To next word	Command-6 (keypad)
To start of line	7 (keypad)
To end of line	1 (keypad)
To previous sentence	Command-7 (keypad)
To next sentence	Command-1 (keypad)
To previous paragraph	Command-8 (keypad)

To move	Press
To next paragraph	Command-2 (keypad)
To top of window	Command-5 (keypad)
To start of document	Command-9 (keypad)
To end of document	Command-3 (keypad)
From window to window	Command-Option-W
To previous cell in table	Command-Option-9 (keypad)
To next cell in table	Command-Option-3 (keypad)
To cell above	Command-Option-8 (keypad)
To cell below	Command-Option-2 (keypad)
To cell to left	Command-Option-4 (keypad)
To cell to right	Command-Option-6 (keypad)

To scroll	Press
One screen up	9 (keypad)
One screen down	3 (keypad)
One line up	Command-Option-[
One line down	Command-Option-/

To select text, press the Shift key while you press one of the key combinations above. The selection will begin at the current position of the insertion point and end where you stop scrolling. To select all the text in a document, press Command-Option-M.

Editing

To	Press
Delete character to left (backward)	Backspace
Delete character to right (forward)	Command-Option-F
Delete previous word	Command-Option-Backspace
Delete next word	Command-Option-G
Find text with the same formats	Command-Option-R

(continued)

To	Press
Insert a new paragraph with the same style	Command-Return
Insert a paragraph above a table	Command-Option-Spacebar
Insert glossary text	Command-Backspace
Insert a formula character	Command-Option-\
Copy text	Command-Option-C
Move text	Command-Option-X
Copy formats	Command-Option-V
Copy as a picture	Command-Option-D
Zoom a window	Command-Option-]
Split a window	Command-Option-S
Open a footnote window	Shift-Command-Option-S

Formatting

For these character formats	Press
Bold	Shift-Command-B
Italic	Shift-Command-I
Underline	Shift-Command-U
Word underline	Shift-Command-]
Double underline	Shift-Command-[
Dotted underline	Shift-Command-\
Strikethrough	Shift-Command-/
Outline	Shift-Command-D
Shadow	Shift-Command-W
Small caps	Shift-Command-H
All caps	Shift-Command-K
Hidden text	Shift-Command-X
Plain text	Shift-Command-Z

Note: To apply the formats above as you type, press the key combination to turn on the format, type the text, and press the key combination again to turn off the format.

To change to this character format	Press
Another font	Shift-Command-E, type font name, then Return or Enter
Larger font size	Shift-Command->
Smaller font size	Shift-Command-<
Symbol font	Shift-Command-Q
Subscript	Shift-Command-minus (−)
Superscript	Shift-Command-plus (+)

For these paragraph formats	Press
Normal paragraph	Shift-Command-P
Change style	Shift-Command-S
Flush left	Shift-Command-L
Flush right	Shift-Command-R
Centered	Shift-Command-C
Justified	Shift-Command-J
First-line indent	Shift-Command-F
Hanging indent	Shift-Command-T
Nest paragraph	Shift-Command-N
Unnest paragraph	Shift-Command-M
Double spacing	Shift-Command-Y
Open spacing	Shift-Command-O

Outlining

To	Press
Promote a heading	Left arrow
Demote a heading	Right arrow
Move heading up	Up arrow
Move heading down	Down arrow
Demote heading to body text	Command-Right arrow
Expand text	+ (keypad)
Collapse text	− (keypad)

(continued)

To	Press
Display all headings and body text	* (keypad)
Display first line only	= (keypad)
Display formatting	/ (keypad)

Working in Page View

To move	Press
To previous text area	Command-Option-9 (keypad)
To next text area	Command-Option-3 (keypad)
To text area above	Command-Option-8 (keypad)
To text area below	Command-Option-2 (keypad)
To text area to left	Command-Option-4 (keypad)
To text area to right	Command-Option-6 (keypad)

Using the Extended Keyboard

If you are using Apple's Extended Keyboard, you'll notice that Word provides additional keyboard equivalents for commands on the menus to allow you to use the function keys (F1, F2, and so on). You can also use the following keys in addition to those listed on the menus (commands are listed in alphabetic order regardless of their menus):

To choose	Press
[Format] Bold	F10
[Format] Character	F14
[Format] Italic	F11
[File] New	F5
[File] Open	F6
[Format] Outline	Shift-F11
[Document] Outlining	Shift-F13
[Document] Page View	F13

To choose	Press
[Format] Paragraph	Shift-F14
[Format] Plain For Style	F9
[Format] Plain Text	Shift-F9
[File] Print	F8
[File] Print Preview	Option-F13
[File] Save	F7
[Format] Shadow	Option-F11
[Utilities] Spelling	F15
[Format] Underline	F12
[Edit] Undo	F1

Index to Menu Commands

Across from each command name is the heading or headings under which you can find information about the command. Menus are listed alphabetically, and commands within each menu are listed alphabetically.

Command	Heading(s)
[Document] menu	
Footnote	Footnotes
Insert Graphics	Graphics
Insert Index Entry	Indexing
Insert Page Break	Page breaks
Insert Table	Tables
Insert TOC Entry	Table of contents
Open Footer	Headers and footers
Open Header	Headers and footers
Outlining	Outlining
Page View	Page View
Repaginate Now	Page breaks
[Edit] menu	
Again	Repeating commands
Clear	Deleting tables and cells, Deleting text
Commands	Customizing Word
Copy	Copying formats, Copying text
Cut	Deleting tables and cells, Deleting text
Glossary	Glossary
Paste	Copying text
Paste Link	QuickSwitch
Preferences	Preferences
Short Menus	Full menus

(continued)

Command	Heading(s)
Show ¶	Symbols
Table	Tables
Undo	Undoing
Update Link	QuickSwitch

[File] menu

Close	Closing a document
Delete	Deleting documents
New	Opening a document
Open	Opening a document
Open Mail	Mail
Page Setup	Printing a document
Print	Printing a document, Printers
Print Merge	Print merge
Print Preview	Print Preview
Quit	Quitting Word
Save	Saving a document
Save As	Saving a document
Send Mail	Mail

*[Font] menu**

9 Point	Formatting characters
10 Point	Formatting characters
12 Point	Formatting characters
.	
.	
Chicago	Formatting characters
Courier	Formatting characters
Geneva	Formatting characters
.	
.	

[Format] menu

Bold	Formatting characters
Cells	Tables

*Commands in the Font menu vary depending on which fonts and font sizes you have installed from the System disk.

Command	Heading(s)
Character	Formatting, Formatting characters
Define Styles	Defining a style, Redefining a style, Styles
Document	Formatting, Formatting documents
Italic	Formatting characters
Outline	Formatting characters
Paragraph	Formatting, Formatting paragraphs
Plain For Style	Formatting, Redefining a style
Plain Text	Formatting characters
Position	Positioning paragraphs
Section	Formatting, Formatting sections
Shadow	Formatting characters
Show Ruler	Ruler
Styles	Applying a style, Styles
Underline	Formatting characters

[Utilities] menu

Command	Heading(s)
Calculate	Math
Change	Searching and replacing
Find	Searching and replacing
Find Again	Searching and replacing
Go Back	Scrolling
Go To	Scrolling
Hyphenate	Hyphenating
Index	Indexing
Renumber	Numbering paragraphs
Sort	Sorting
Spelling	Spell checking
Table of Contents	Table of contents
Word Count	Counting

[Window] menu

Command	Heading(s)
Help	Help
Command	Heading(s)
New Window	Windows
Show Clipboard	Clipboard

Alphabetic Index to Commands

Across from each command name is the heading or headings under which you can find information about the command. Commands are listed alphabetically, regardless of the menus in which they appear.

Command	Heading(s)
9 Point	Formatting characters
10 Point	Formatting characters
12 Point	Formatting characters
Again	Repeating commands
Bold	Formatting characters
Calculate	Math
Cells	Tables
Change	Searching and replacing
Character	Formatting, Formatting characters
Chicago	Formatting characters
Clear	Deleting tables and cells, Deleting text
Close	Closing a document
Commands	Customizing Word
Copy	Copying formats, Copying text
Courier	Formatting characters
Cut	Deleting tables and cells, Deleting text
Define Styles	Defining a style, Redefining a style, Styles
Delete	Deleting documents, Deleting tables and cells, Deleting text
Document	Formatting, Formatting documents
Find	Searching and replacing
Find Again	Searching and replacing

(continued)

(Note: Commands in the Font menu vary depending on which fonts and font sizes you have installed from the System disk.)

Command	Heading(s)
Footnote	Footnotes
Geneva	Formatting characters
Glossary	Glossary
Go Back	Scrolling
Go To	Scrolling
Help	Help
Hyphenate	Hyphenating
Index	Indexing
Insert Graphics	Graphics
Insert Index Entry	Indexing
Insert Page Break	Page breaks
Insert Table	Tables
Insert TOC Entry	Table of contents
Italic	Formatting characters
New	Opening a document
New Window	Windows
Open	Opening a document
Open Footer	Headers and footers
Open Header	Headers and footers
Open Mail	Mail
Outline	Formatting characters
Outlining	Outlining
Page Setup	Printing a document
Page View	Page View
Paragraph	Formatting, Formatting paragraphs
Paste	Copying text
Paste Link	QuickSwitch
Plain For Style	Formatting, Redefining a style
Plain Text	Formatting characters
Position	Positioning paragraphs
Preferences	Preferences
Print	Printing a document, Printers
Print Merge	Print merge
Print Preview	Print Preview

Command	Heading(s)
Quit	Quitting Word
Renumber	Numbering paragraphs
Repaginate Now	Page breaks
Save	Saving a document
Save As	Saving a document
Section	Formatting, Formatting sections
Send Mail	Mail
Shadow	Formatting characters
Short Menus	Full menus
Show ¶	Symbols
Show Clipboard	Clipboard
Show Ruler	Ruler
Sort	Sorting
Spelling	Spell checking
Styles	Applying a style, Styles
Table	Tables
Table of Contents	Table of contents
Underline	Formatting characters
Undo	Undoing
Update Link	QuickSwitch
Word Count	Counting

OTHER TITLES FROM MICROSOFT PRESS

THE APPLE® MACINTOSH® BOOK, 3rd edition
Cary Lu

"The one Macintosh book you'd choose if you could have only one. Virtually anything you might want to know at any level is here."   **MACazine**

The classic book that accompanied the introduction of the Mac in 1984 is back again and thoroughly updated to include information the Mac II, SE, and Plus. THE APPLE MACINTOSH BOOK provides an authoritative and comprehensive look at the Mac's design philosophy, architecture, hardware and software options, and significant user issues. Cary Lu covers selecting the right Mac, uses of the Mac, internal hardware expansion, mass-storage options, local area networks, and more. If you currently use a Mac or expect to use one, you need this book.

416 pages, softcover $21.95   Order Code: 86-96213

WORKING WITH WORD, 2nd ed.
The Definitive Guide to Microsoft® Word on the Apple® Macintosh®
Chris Kinata and Gordon McComb

When you are ready to go beyond simple word processing with Microsoft Word for the Macintosh, this is *the* book of choice. Now updated for version 4, it's filled with inside advice, detailed information, and tutorials on every software feature. Included are scores of excellent tips — many not in the documentation — designed to add power and functionality, no matter what kind of printed documents you want to create. Topics cover: desktop publishing with Word; integrating graphics into a Word document and wrapping text around them; customizing menus and retrieving lost files; linking Word with other applications; optimizing memory management; creating spreadsheetlike tables; and working with lists and multiple columns. Also included are blueprints for newsletters, multicolumn brochures, correspondence, and reports. WORKING WITH WORD is the best, most complete, and most up-to-date book on Microsoft Word available.

752 pages, softcover $21.95   Order Code: 86-96957

EXCEL IN BUSINESS
Number-Crunching Power on the Apple® Macintosh®
Douglas Cobb and The Cobb Group

"The definitive guide to Excel on the Macintosh... an outstanding reference, for its readability and detail."   **Computer Book Review**

Microsoft Excel, the powerful integrated spreadsheet, database, and graphics package, lets you perform a variety of tasks for business and personal use. EXCEL IN BUSINESS will help beginners to advanced users access Excel's capabilities in the most efficient way. The authors include practical applications for learning how to produce spreadsheets and graphics; how to work with databases; how to master macros; how to link Excel to other programs. Packed with scores of tutorials and dozens of tips. Now updated to version 1.5.

816 pages, softcover $24.95   Order Code: 86-95314

DOUG COBB'S TIPS FOR MICROSOFT® EXCEL
The Cobb Group: Douglas Cobb, Judy Mynhier, Gena Berg Cobb

"Highlights the not-so-obvious things the average user ought to know about using Excel."   **Computer Book Review**

Douglas Cobb and The Cobb Group have assembled a collection of creative, timesaving tips that extract optimum performance from Microsoft Excel. The book is designed for quick lookups and reference, and each tip includes a ready-to-implement example and concise explanation. You'll discover valuable information about worksheets, databases, graphics, command macros, and user-defined functions.

384 pages, softcover $19.95   Order Code: 86-95660

THE NEW WRITER
Techniques for Writing Well with a Computer
Joan P. Mitchell

"If you have any writing to do in your life — anything (from letters to business reports) — here's the book for you and your computer."   **The Tulsa World**

THE NEW WRITER, written by an experienced writing instructor, shows you how to master process writing and how to improve your overall writing skills. Mitchell tells you how to use the computer to work successfully through all the basic writing steps. You will learn how to brainstorm and analyze, edit and revise, communicate ideas visually as well as verbally, and use special computer tools like idea processors, outliners, and spell checkers to produce clear expository works.

256 pages, softcover $8.95   Order Code: 86-95900

DESKTOP PUBLISHING BY DESIGN
Blueprints for Page Layout Using Aldus® PageMaker®
on IBM® and Apple® Macintosh® Computers
Ronnie Shushan and Don Wright

DESKTOP PUBLISHING BY DESIGN includes a variety of versatile, hands-on projects that use the full capabilities of PageMaker for the lastest IBM and Macintosh versions. The authors emphasize the effective use of design elements — typeface, page layout, and graphics to help you create professional looking newsletters, brochures, catalogs, manuals, directories, even magazines. You will learn not only how to manipulate and manage PageMaker, but how to produce exciting, professional pieces with ease.

400 pages, softcover $19.95   Order Code: 86-96460

The manuscript for this book was prepared and submitted to Microsoft Press in electronic form. Text files were processed and formatted using Microsoft Word.

Cover design by Thomas A. Draper
Interior text design by Greg Hickman
Principal typography by Lisa Iversen
Color separations by Wescan Color Corporation

Text composition by Microsoft Press in Times Roman with display in Times Roman Bold, using the Magna composition system and the Linotronic 300 laser imagesetter.